TROUBLE FOR YOUR THOUGHTS

KARI LEE TOWNSEND

OUVERTESTI BOOKS

To all the mamas out there, I hope you know how much you're loved! Keep fighting and keep the faith. I am lucky to have two amazing women in my life: my mama Marion Harmon and mama-in-law Joan Townsend.

To my mama: thank you for loving me unconditionally and for raising me to know right from wrong, to treat people with kindness, to love myself, to be strong and confident, to know how to raise my own children, and to know what it takes to have a happy marriage and how to make it work. Thank you for always being there for me and your grandchildren. You're the strongest, most resilient fighter I've ever known. I love you more than words can say.

To my mama-in-law: thank you for accepting me into your life wholeheartedly and for loving me like one of your own, for raising such a great man I call my own, for cherishing your grandchildren and letting them know what family means, for being a light in all our lives, and for bringing laughter and happiness to every get-together. You're resilient and tough and find a way to overcome life's obstacles like no other. I love you more than words can say.

I. Am. Blessed.

"I can't believe the puppies are three months old already," I said to Jaz Alvarez as we got ready to open her clothing boutique, *Full Disclosure*.

She had a full-time cleaning crew, but she was a perfectionist like me, overseeing every detail. I helped her by straightening the clothing racks, while she fluffed the decorative pin striped pillows on the burgundy microfiber sofa and matching love seat in the sitting area next to the dressing rooms.

"Twelve weeks of terror. Makes me second guess having babies if they're anything like raising puppies." Jaz put the drawer in the cash register and then walked over to turn on the lights to the *Open* sign.

Jaz and I had known each other since we were little, but we were complete opposites. She was model-tall with thick, honey-brown curls, amber eyes, and striking features. While I was average height with golden-blonde hair, green eyes, and curves. She was outgoing, while I was an introvert, yet we were the perfect complements and the best of friends.

I rented the loft in her shop to create my *Kalli Originals* lingerie designs. They were displayed at *Inter-*

ludes in New York City, but also right here in Clearview, our quaint little town in Connecticut.

"I hear you." I laughed. "Willow is an angel, and she's housebroken already, but she's still not sleeping through the night. I'm so tired all the time."

"Armani isn't sleeping through the night either, and he's marking everything in sight in our brand-new house." Jaz's lips twisted into a frown. "I am not a happy camper with him, and neither is Boomer."

Detective Boomer Matheson and Jaz were engaged. They just bought their first house, and their dream barn wedding is in August, which I can't believe is a month away. Boomer and my fiancé, Detective Nik Stevens, were partners. Boomer and Jaz rescued two female full-size, purebred black poodles, Chanel and Versace, when their owners were no longer able to take care of them.

While Nik and I had my prissy calico cat, Priscilla, and his big, slobbery Saint Bernard, Wolfgang. We'd remodeled our house, knocking down the walls between our apartments and making both our places one big home.

When Wolfgang got loose with the poodle twins, each female gave birth to a large litter of Saint Berdoodles, overwhelming us all. Jaz and Boomer had found homes for all of them except two. They kept the largest male, Armani, while Nik and I kept the runt of the litter—a female we named Willow.

"I'm just so glad you're home," Jaz said, giving me a quick hug. "It helps to have someone around who gets it."

"You and me both. I loved spending time with Sunny and Mitch, but I never intended to be in Divinity for so long. That was the longest two months of my life. I really thought I was going to jail for murder."

"Um, yeah, I'm not letting you leave me again. Next time, Sunny will just have to come to Clearview."

"Amen to that. Hopefully, my days of drama are in the past. I could use a little R&R after what the mamas put us through."

"I can't believe they followed you to Divinity ... actually, yes, I can. Greek mamas on a mission are a force to be reckoned with. It sounds like their three act plays about you and Nik were a hoot."

"I can laugh about it now, but trust me, it wasn't funny at the time." I groaned, rubbing my temples as I tried to erase the embarrassing memories.

I was adopted into a big, fat Greek family and my parents only child. Or at least I *was* their only child. But when my birth mother was murdered and Ma found out I had a half-brother named Jasper, she adopted him as well.

He was a grown man—twenty-seven years old—but that didn't matter one bit to my ma.

I had to admit it was nice having someone to share the spotlight with. And now that my nice half-Greek boy Nik had proposed—or rather, I did ... we were still debating whose proposal counted—we were officially engaged. The pressure to meet a nice Greek boy and give my parents grandbabies had lessened somewhat, thank Zeus.

Now they were focused on finding Jasper a Nice Greek girl. He wasn't any more Greek than I was, but that didn't matter. He was a Ballas now, and that was Greek enough. While I was adopted as a baby, Jasper had grown up in the foster system alone. He was loving every minute of being a Ballas and was a reminder every day for me to be thankful for what I had.

Even though they drove me crazy!

Speaking of crazy ... the bells over the door jingled

and in breezed the Three Act Trio: my ma Ophelia, my aunt Tasoula, and Nik's ma Chloe.

Ma was a larger-than-life Greek mama who owned *Aphrodite's* restaurant with my pop. She had a big poof of teased black hair she wore in a beehive. She wore flashy polyester pants, believed Aloe could cure everything, and was constantly trying to fix my quirks.

Aunt Tasoula was her widowed younger sister who dressed like she was half her age with long black extensions and clothes two sizes too tight. She owned a hair salon and spa called *Hera's Halo* and her on-again-off-again boyfriend was the local hardware store owner, Tate Hemsworth.

Meanwhile, Chloe Pagonis was chic and sophisticated. She'd married Bjorn Stevens, a blond-haired, blue-eyed Scandinavian Viking, but their marriage hadn't lasted. Nik inherited his mother's good looks, as well as his father's brilliant blue eyes and massive size. Currently, Chloe was dating Nik and Boomer's dashing captain, Quincy Crenshaw, with his salt and pepper hair and steel-gray eyes, but she'd never quite gotten over Bjorn.

"Ah, there's my beautiful brides." Ma swooped in for a big hug. *You too thin. How you gonna make babies with no meat on you bones?*

"Hi, Ma." I stepped back so I wouldn't have to hear her thoughts. "What brings you by the shop?"

I discreetly sanitized my hands with the small bottle of hand sanitizer I kept in my pocket. Ever since a freak accident happened where I fell out of my loft and hit my head, I had been able to read people's minds but only when touching them—a nightmare for an OCD germaphobe like me.

"What? We no welcome now that you engaged?" Aunt Tasoula's hand fluttered to her bedazzled chest in time with her rapidly blinking eye lashes. "Oh, woe is me. They no need us anymore."

"We always need you," Jaz interjected. "Why, Kalli and I were just talking about how helpful you all were in her time of need not long ago."

I shot Jaz a *seriously* stare, and she returned an *I'm-sorry-I-panicked* look.

"I'm glad to hear that," Chloe said, clapping her hands. "So, how are your wedding plans, Jaz?"

"All done." Jaz beamed.

"And you?" Chloe asked as the trio turned their eyes on me.

"Oh, well, I haven't exactly started." The acid began to form in my stomach, and I briefly feared what it was doing to my insides.

"That what we afraid of." Ma tsked, shaking her head.

"You no worry." Aunt Tasoula nodded once. "We help you knot the tie." She winked. "I good at that."

And *that* was what *I* was afraid of ... so much for no more drama.

~

"YOU READY TO GO, BALLAS," Nik asked on Sunday morning, looking dashing in his sport coat and jeans. He was so tall with thick, wavy coffee-colored hair, olive skin, a heavily whiskered face, and piercing blue eyes. He winked at me. "You know how the mamas get if we're late for service."

"Do we have to?" I moaned. "If I have to listen to one more piece of advice on what we should do for our wedding, I'm going to lose it. Can't we just enjoy being engaged for at least a little bit?"

"Not with Greek mamas." He shook his head, his

chiseled features forming a serious expression as he arched an eyebrow at me. "If they don't have something to fuss about, they get into trouble."

"Well, then, I know what I'm praying for in church today."

"What's that?"

"Something to fuss about other than us."

He laughed. "I'll do the same. We need all the prayers we can get. Even more reason not to be late, especially if we want Father Papadopoulos to marry us." He grabbed the keys, turned a light on, turned on some sounds-of-nature music, filled the water bowls, then headed out to the car.

Just like my best friend, I'd chosen a complete opposite for my life partner as well. Detective Dreamy was outgoing and confident with a devil-may-care attitude. When he was Nik, he was the nice guy. When he was Nikos, he was the smug Greek. When he was Detective Stevens, he was all business.

And all of them together were mine.

I set Willow on her dog bed in a small, gated area with water and toys to keep her safe while we were gone. Of course, the little stinker curled right up and went to sleep now that it was daylight.

I sighed, smoothing my skirt and making sure my standard chignon was perfectly in place.

Prissy leapt up high to her cat perch, far away from Wolfgang. Speaking of the devil, he looked up at me with his big brown eyes and whined.

"Okay, big fella, I'll pet you, but you know the rule. Don't slobber on me." I shuddered just thinking about how many germs were in his saliva.

He sat perfectly still as I stroked his massive head, then I sanitized my hands, of course. I did cave and winked at him as I blew him a kiss.

If dogs could smile, he gave me a big one and then curled up on the floor outside of Willow's pen to watch over her.

"Good boy." I locked up and joined Nik outside in the car.

Five minutes later, we arrived at *Holy Trinity Greek Orthodox Church*. Father Papadopoulos and Sister Philothea—lover of God—stood just outside the church with the doors opened wide in a welcoming gesture.

The sun was out today, but the ground was saturated with water after the late-spring-early-summer floods. Of course, the mamas took it as a sign that Mother Nature wasn't happy with the citizens of Clearview.

We headed up to the church doors.

"Morning, Father," Nik said. "Good to see you, Sister."

"Good morning, Nikos." Father smiled wide, a twinkle in his eyes. "Kalliope, it's been a while, what with your unexpected delay in Divinity. Your mama told me all about it. Glad to see you here. I'm sure you have much to pray about."

"Oh, I sure do," I ground out through my teeth but kept that bright wide smile in place as I nodded to the sister.

As we entered the church, the vision before me calmed me as it always did. The walls were lined with gold icons and intricate frescoes depicting scenes from the Bible. Sunlight streamed in through the tall windows, casting a warm glow on the vibrant rugs and tapestries that adorned the floors and walls.

The smell of incense filled my nostrils, mingling with the scent of fresh flowers and the warmth of candle wax. It was a comforting and familiar smell, one that reminded me of my childhood and holidays spent at church. The grandeur of the church was matched only by the warmth and love emanating from its parishioners who greeted us with open arms and holy kisses.

It was a place of peace and beauty.

My mouth watered as I caught a whiff of the delicious aromas coming from the nearby kitchen, where the church ladies were cooking up traditional Greek dishes for the upcoming festival. The marble floor was cool beneath my feet as we found our families' pew and took our seats.

IN THE GREEK ORTHODOX RELIGION, the service lasted one and a half to two hours. The Divine Liturgy was often chanted or sung in the Greek language, with minimal spoken parts. Jasper was still struggling to learn it so he could keep up.

Communion was offered with a spoon containing both the bread and wine combined. Icons of flat stylized images were used extensively and played a central role in worship with congregants bowing and kissing to venerate the icons.

Father Papadopoulos faced the altar, away from the congregation, to emphasize worship directed toward God. The Incense that had greeted me at the door was used heavily, symbolizing prayers rising to heaven, with more frequent crossing and bowing. The entire liturgy was viewed as deeply sacramental, with greater emphasis placed on preparation like fasting and confession for participating in the Eucharist. Both our families were very involved, especially the mamas.

When the service was over, we all headed outside,

ready to go to Ma and Pop's house for our Sunday brunch in their backyard. Well, it was called a back-yard, but it was more like a Greek museum, containing a gazebo, marble statues, and even a water fountain. We didn't get far because of the sight before us.

Oh, my Zeus ... be careful what you wish—er pray —for.

Tons of little snakes were all over the church grounds!

"Oh, woe is me ... the legend has found us," Aunt Tasoula wailed, hopping and dancing around in a cir-cle, trying not to step on any.

"Right!" Ma made the sign of the cross, then made shooing motions with her hands. "That mean trouble coming."

"We must be like nuns and protect our families." Chloe fingered her rosary, chanting prayers to the gods.

Being Greek, we'd grown up hearing about all of the legends throughout history. Every year at the church of the Virgin Mary in Markopoulo village in Greece, little snakes appeared inside and outside of the church, then disappeared at the end of the day. The legend said once when pirates attacked the monastery, nuns prayed to be rescued and snakes ap-peared, chasing the pirates away. Villagers tried to touch them to bring good luck to their families.

But legends were just that ... legends. And this one had never happened in Clearview.

"The legend happens in Greece, not here. Besides, it says this happens on August fifteenth. That's over two weeks away," I pointed out logically.

They ignored me, walking off with their heads bent close and their hands gesturing wildly.

I sighed. "I'd say they have something new to fuss about."

Nik frowned, transforming into Detective Stevens. "And that worries me far more than their meddling in our wedding plans ever did."

No truer words had ever been spoken ...

2

Captain Crenshaw stood tall and poised on the front steps of *Holy Trinity Greek Orthodox Church*, his presence commanding attention. He engaged in an intense discussion with Father Papadopoulos, a kindly man with warm eyes and a gentle smile, and Sister Philothea—who was new to the parish—her serene face betraying none of the worry that seemed to plague Mayor Flynn Zimmerman.

The mayor herself was a force to be reckoned with, her expressive hands waving frantically as she spoke. Flynn exuded an air of sophistication with her short, gray streaked hair and no-nonsense attitude. Since taking office, she had made it her mission to clean up the streets of Clearview and prove herself to the town. With the county fair just around the corner, she surely didn't need another scandal on her hands.

As we waited for herpetologist Natalie Rodriguez to finish assessing the situation, Detective Matheson joined Nik and me on the church grounds. Boomer—a towering man with unruly russet colored hair and hazel eyes—shuddered in disgust as he sidestepped a snake that slithered by.

"I hate snakes," he muttered.

Nik shrugged nonchalantly. "I don't mind them. When I was little, my pop had several. He was always fascinated by them, and his best friend was an expert on them."

"These look pretty harmless." I cringed as I looked around at the multitude of snakes surrounding us, wondering what kind of diseases they might carry. "There are an awful lot of them, though."

Finally, Natalie finished putting away her supplies in her company truck before walking over to join us. I'd never met her. She covered the entire county and didn't live in Clearview. She was petite and attractive with short dark curly hair that framed her face. Despite being in her fifties, she exuded youthfulness and energy as she greeted Nik with a handshake.

"Detective Stevens," she said warmly. "And this must be your partner, Detective Matheson," she added, turning to Boomer and shaking his hand.

"What could have caused this?" Boomer asked, gesturing towards the mass of snakes slithering around us. "That legend?"

"What legend?" Natalie furrowed her brow in confusion.

"They're talking about an ancient Greek legend called the Virgin Mary Snakes in Cephalonia, but it's never happened in the United States that I know of," I interjected, offering my hand to shake hers as well. "I'm Kalli Ballas, Detective Stevens' fiancé."

Natalie smiled as she shook my hand. *Lucky you.* "So, tell me then, what does this Greek legend have to do with these snakes?"

I dropped her hand and slipped mine into the pockets of my jacket, twirling my fidget ring until I could sanitize my hands without offending anyone.

"Well, in ancient Greece, Nuns prayed for help from pirates in Cephalonia, and snakes appeared at their church to scare them away." I held my hands up. "Greeks are always looking for signs. Some people believe that if snakes appear, it means there's danger headed our way."

Natalie raised an eyebrow skeptically. "I don't know about any danger, but I can tell you that these snakes have nothing to do with some silly legend."

Don't let the mamas hear you. I raised a brow but kept my thought to myself.

"Then why are the snakes here?" Nik chimed in, all business, his gaze scanning the area nonstop.

"Well, it's a bit of a perfect storm situation," Natalie began as she bent over and picked one up.

Boomer hopped a foot back and a strangled yelp escaped his lips.

Natalie eyed him curiously before showing us all the snake a little closer ... except for Boomer. "These are Eastern Garter snakes. They tend to appear in gardens and grassy areas in this area. They're more visible during breeding season in late spring and early summer. And lately, we've had extreme weather with all the floods which has pushed them out of their usual habitats and onto higher ground."

Boomer cleared his throat and muttered again, "I hate snakes."

"Fortunately, these ones are harmless and non-venomous," Natalie reassured him, setting the snake back down.

Nik glanced at Captain Crenshaw and Mayor Zimmerman who were still on the church steps before looking Natalie in the eyes. "What can be done to remove them as quickly as possible?"

"While these snakes aren't endangered, they are

beneficial to the ecosystem," Natalie explained. "It's important not to harm them if possible."

"The church holds a Big Greek Bake sale during the county fair with proceeds going to charities and various projects that benefit the town. While Greek people might consider the snakes good luck, I doubt tourists will. An infestation of snakes could scare people away. The town relies on fund raisers like these," Boomer added, his eyes alert.

"We could try removing their food source of insects and rodents by trimming the grass and shrubs, clearing out any debris, rockpiles, woodpiles, and making the garden fence snake-proof."

"The grounds keeper, Dale, can help with that," Nik said.

"The church is old, so we'll also need to block and seal any gaps, holes, or cracks in the church's structure with caulk or wire mesh so the snakes can't get inside," Natalie continued, looking at the notes she'd written during her assessment.

"The maintenance man, Cole, can help with that," Boomer added.

"Using safe, non-toxic repellents like sulfur, clove oil, and cinnamon oil sprinkled around the perimeter of the property can also be effective," Natalie added.

"It's a Greek church. I'm sure the parishioners can help with that," I said.

"Good." Natalie nodded. "And finally, fixing any leaking pipes, hoses, or standing water will help dry out the grounds and discourage the snakes from staying."

"Kalli's cousin, Yanni, is the one who did the landscaping for the church," Jaz chimed in. "I'm sure he could help fix it since his reputation is on the line."

"What if none of this works?" I spoke up, gnawing my bottom lip.."

"If all else fails, we can use snake grabbers and nets to safely catch and relocate them away from the property."

As if the very thought of snake grabbers were terrifying, Boomer's face twisted into an expression of sheer horror. His eyes widened and his mouth hung open in disbelief. "Just ... what do those look like? Because I'm not getting closer than six feet to any snakes."

"I suspect they're like long tongs, honey," Jaz reassured him.

"Correct," Natalie said, her voice calm and soothing like a gentle breeze on a warm summer day and not the darkening sky and increased wind of the moment. "Not much to be afraid of unless you have a phobia," she added.

"Great, just great," Boomer retorted, shaking out his arms as if ready for the horn to go off at the start of a race. He stood fidgety, ready to bolt under the threat of snakes. "I have enough to deal with without having to grapple with giant tongs and slithering creatures. What's next? An infestation of spiders?"

"Don't put that out into the universe, please," I exclaimed, shaking my head vigorously. The mere thought of spiders made my skin crawl. "Ma already thinks the snakes are a sign of pure evil headed our way. She would think spiders were an omen of Armageddon."

"We need to focus," Nik said, his no-nonsense detective brow furrowing. His deep voice rumbled through the air like distant thunder, commanding attention. "We need to get to the bottom of the infestation before the mamas stage an intervention involving holy water or worse."

"He has a point," I said, nodding in agreement.

"Right, so let's get our priorities straight," Boomer said, looking from Nik to me and back again. His tone was serious and determined as he spoke. "We need a plan. First, we let Natalie handle how to get rid of the snakes—safely, of course—and then we deal with the Greek mamas."

"I can already hear them," I groaned, picturing Ma whipping a rosary around like a lasso, and Aunt Tasoula playing a pungi to charm the snakes with its hypnotic tone. "The last thing we need is them showing up with their healing oils and sacramental candles, trying to cleanse the church grounds."

Natalie chuckled softly, her laugh easing the tension somewhat. "You'd be surprised what people will do when superstition takes hold. If these mamas of yours are as superstitious as you say and think those snakes are bad omens, this situation could escalate quickly into something worse." She glanced toward the church entrance where Father Papadopoulos was still deep in conversation with the mayor and Captain Crenshaw.

"Well, if it comes down to holy water versus snake grabbers," Boomer said, "I'm all for the water."

"I'll talk with Father and see what he wants me to do then go from there." Natalie nodded once before heading over to the church steps.

"This doesn't look good." Nik frowned, his usually stoic face creased with worry.

"What else could possibly go wrong?" I shrugged, trying to brush off my growing sense of unease.

Suddenly, the sky darkened even more, blotting out the sun and casting shadows across the town. The wind picked up, rustling through leaves and stirring up dust on the streets, causing the snakes to slither in a frenzy, and people to run away screaming.

In the distance, the thunder sounded threatening.

Great, just what Clearview needed ... more rain.

The air was heavy, foreboding. Suddenly I had the most uneasy feeling settle over me. Like a storm brewing within me as well as above us. I blinked rapidly, trying to shake off this strange intuition.

Maybe trouble was headed our way sooner than we thought.

~

LITERALLY THAT NIGHT, our families and friends had agreed to skip brunch after a very long day figuring out what to do about the snakes. Not to mention, the weather was getting worse. Instead, we headed to my parents' authentic Greek restaurant, *Aphrodite's*.

My parents had just remodeled the restaurant, with Jasper's help, adding a large patio with music and lights outside for the warmer months. Ma still wanted to expand with another restaurant, but for now she was content with upgrades to her baby.

The exterior of *Aphrodite's* was a charming blend of white stone walls, with intricate patterns and designs, and a bright blue awning that proudly displayed the restaurant's name. The entrance was marked by a large wooden door with Greek symbols carved into it and tall columns on both sides topped with ornate carvings of Greek gods.

As we entered the restaurant, the coolness of the air-conditioning was a little chilly since the rain had started. The walls were adorned with art and photographs of Greece and the Mediterranean coast, giving off a warm and welcoming atmosphere. The tables were covered with white tablecloths with red and blue accents and marble statues of Greek gods and goddesses throughout the restaurant. At the center of it all was the restaurant's namesake, Aphrodite, radiating beauty and love to all who dined within her walls.

The aroma of sizzling meats, herbs, and spices filled the air. The distinct scents of olive oil, garlic, and oregano as well as freshly baked bread and desserts wafted out the door, inviting all who passed by to come in and experience the rich flavors of Greece. The menu boasted a variety of traditional Greek dishes, from gyros to souvlaki and moussaka, offering a burst of bold flavors.

The sound of Greek music filled the room, lively and upbeat. The tables and chairs were made of dark wood, polished to a shine. The fabric on the chairs was soft and plush, inviting you to sit down and stay a while. The plates and silverware had intricate designs, adding to the authenticity of the restaurant.

Nik's eyes widened in awe as he surveyed the lavish renovations done by my parents.

I led him to our reserved table, carefully avoiding any contact with the other patrons. My parents knew my quirks and always made sure everything was perfect for me, from the cleanliness of the kitchen to providing my own sanitized utensils.

"Wow, your parents went all out on the renovation," Nik said, looking around impressed.

"I know, right?" I nodded. "Jasper has a great eye, and Ma was only too happy to let him take the lead."

As we sat down, I noticed Nik's ma, Chloe, and Captain Crenshaw sitting with my parents, Aunt Tasoula, and Tate. My cousin, Eleni, served as a waitress while her younger sister, Frona, worked in the back as a dishwasher. Her once bright future had been dimmed by a past incident when she fell off an apple cart, but she still found joy in her simple life with the help of my yiayia Dido.

Frona skipped around with a bin in hand, her pigtails swinging as she sang and cleared tables without regard for whether or not the customers were finished. My yiayia chased after her with an apron tied around her waist and gray hair pulled back tightly in a bun. Leni even offered free desserts to appease any disgruntled diners.

I couldn't help feeling grateful that Nik came from a large Greek family like mine. He understood the drama that came with having such a close-knit community. Our families practically made up half of the town, making it nearly impossible to have a date night without someone showing up uninvited.

As we placed our orders and waited for our drinks, I couldn't resist bringing up the topic of marriage. "So, when do you want to tie the knot?" I asked casually, before taking a sip of my wine.

Nik's response caught me off guard as he slowly took a sip of his whiskey before answering. "I don't know ... with Willow still not sleeping through the night and now this snake infestation, it's hard to think about that right now."

Part of me wished that he didn't know about my ability to read minds. If I touched him, he would know that I just wanted to hear his true thoughts. "I understand, it's a lot to think about. I was just curious."

"I love you, Ballas," he said with such sincerity that I didn't doubt his words for a second.

"I love you too, Detective." I winked playfully, but deep down, I couldn't help wondering if he was dragging his feet. Up until recently, he had been the one pressuring me to set a date.

Before we could continue our conversation, Leni arrived with our food and warned us to eat quickly before Frona got her hands on it. We laughed and fell into silence as we enjoyed our meals, grateful for this moment of peace amidst the craziness of our families.

My parents had been married forever, while his had gotten divorced when he was young and never married again. His father had moved away to London and then later to Norway on a business venture, while his mother stayed in New York only moving to Connecticut after Nik did. Many of the Pagonis clan followed suit.

Since then, his parents had each gone through several romances, but they were happy. Nik had proposed, so I assumed he still wanted to get married, but he didn't seem to be in a rush. I had never wanted to get married, but he had won me over.

Now he seemed to be the one getting cold feet.

I was probably overthinking things like I usually did. There would be plenty of time to set a date. Once we got these snakes taken care of, peace would return to Clearview. What else could possibly go wrong?

Just then the door swung open, and a blond-haired giant stormed in, his thick long hair and clothes wet from the tempest still raging outside. Men cleared a path, women swooned, and the massive man on a mission took long, purposeful strides until he came to a stop before my parents' table.

The restaurant fell into silence.

Ma's eyes widened, her eyelids blinking like windshield wipers on high.

Aunt Tasoula fanned her flushed face, her lips opening and closing like a blowfish.

A shocked Chloe Pagonis sputtered, "B-Bjorn? What are you doing here?"

I blinked. Nik's father looked like Thor's daddy, but he carried a red rose instead of a hammer.

"You and I, my skatt, need to talk." He thrust out the rose and held it before her.

Captain Crenshaw frowned.

"Did he just call your ma a name?" I whispered to Nik.

Nik groaned. "No, he used a term of endearment. This can't be good."

Chloe pushed the rose aside and thrust her nose in the air, sitting up ramrod straight. "You have no right to call me your treasure." Her hands moved in time with her lips. "You give that up over twenty years ago."

"Things change." Bjorn shrugged his massive shoulders. "I miss you, Elskling."

"You no call me darling, either." Chloe crossed her arms over her chest.

"Chloe, what's going on?" Quincy asked.

"You no worry, Agapi mou." She winked at the captain and squeezed his hand. "I handle my ex-husband."

"Your *love*?" Bjorn turned his sapphire blue eyes so like Nik's onto Quincy. "Who is this man?"

Quincy leveled steel-gray eyes onto Bjorn, a muscle in his jaw flexing.

Chloe looked Bjorn square in the eyes and firmly replied, "My fiancé."

A gasp rang out in the room.

"Does this mean you say yes?" Quincy looked at her skeptically.

"Yes. I done thinking it over. I will marry you," she

said, but her eyes were still fixed on Bjorn with a triumphant, smug look on her face.

A laugh rumbled from deep within Bjorn's broad chest before he responded with a soft voice, "We're not finished here, Snuppa," the challenge gleaming in his sizzling eyes, "because I'm here to stay."

If I didn't know better, I could have sworn I heard the sound of hissing snakes, because if I wasn't mistaken ... trouble had just arrived.

3

The days following Chloe's shocking announcement were a whirlwind of emotions for both me and Nik. He said that he couldn't shake the feeling that his mother had only agreed to marry Quincy because his father was present.

Neither of them had ever remarried, and Nik admitted his father was a good man and a great father, but a terrible husband. His wandering spirit had led him to constantly seek new adventures, leaving his family behind. Meanwhile, his ma stayed close to her Greek roots and would never dream of leaving her family.

There was also the fact that his *spirit* wasn't the only thing that wandered.

Women loved Bjorn Stevens, and he never could resist them. But that didn't mean that Chloe wasn't the love of his life, just as he was the love of hers. That definitely didn't mean they should get married again.

Poor Nik felt like he was stuck in the middle between his parents as well as his captain. If he'd been stalling in setting a date for our wedding before, he certainly wouldn't be in any hurry to now.

Planning a wedding was a lot of pressure, but *his* hesitation made me nervous. So, Jaz had suggested a much-needed spa day.

I didn't do the spa, but my aunt's salon, *Hera's Halo,* was different. Just like in Ma's restaurant with my special table and sterilized utensils, Aunt Tasoula set aside a special sanitized cape for me in the back.

She was the only one I would let touch my hair.

Hera's Halo was next door to my papou's dry cleaning business. My aunt had decorated her salon with a queen of the gods theme because she believed that every woman was a queen worthy of looking and feeling like one. The chairs were replicas of gold thrones with the capes being like a queen's robe, and the dryers were painted like crowns with precious gems adorning them.

The newest touches were a swing in one corner of the waiting room and a stripper pole in the other, remnants of the wild escapades my aunt had gotten into with the other mamas. In the back, the nail tech, Rosy, was booked solid and so was Perry the masseuse.

Rosy was doing nails for a travel blogger named Emily Nguyen who wrote about unique stories to share with her followers. Jaz was telling her all about the snakes while Perry gave her a massage. I had just taken a seat in Aunt Tasoula's chair, and Ma was reading a magazine, waiting for Chloe.

The bell over the door chimed and in walked a beautiful Greek woman with short, black slicked-back hair, around the same age as the mamas.

Ma gasped, her face beaming and flushed with color. "Y-You Marieta Galanis, the world-renowned Greek chef."

The woman arched a sleek, perfectly shaped eyebrow high and inhaled a deep breath, as if she had grown used to moments like these. "Why, yes I am." She held out her hand. "And who might you be?"

Ma shook her hand and fumbled over her words. "Why, I ... I ..." She looked at my aunt helplessly. "Who am I?"

"You Ophelia Ballas." Aunt Tasoula made the sign of the cross. "Do you lose you marbles? Maybe the snakes take them."

"Snakes?" Marieta's eyes turned sharp as she looked around with curiosity. "You have snakes in here?"

"No here." Aunt Tasoula shook her head hard. "My salon protected by the gods. Snakes at Church." My aunt shuddered.

"Ah, I see. The Greek legend. I grew up hearing about that, too in my hometown." Marieta nodded, accepting that without a second thought. "Never heard of it happening outside of Greece, though. Not a good sign for the church if trouble is coming."

"I'll be there with bells on," Emily said, swinging her burgundy ponytail as she talked. "My followers are going to love this."

"You no bring bells to church. What wrong with you?" Ma frowned at Emily. "You need nice Greek boy to set you straight. I introduce you to my son, Jasper. Okay?"

Emily's eyebrows arched high then puckered. "Okay, I guess ...?"

"Okay. It settled." Ma cleared her throat, taking a sip of cucumber water as she faced Marieta. "I better now. You come to service. Church be fine." She nodded once, hard, her beehive bobbing like a bobble head. "What bring you to Clearview?"

"I'm on tour, promoting my television show, *Hades' Kitchen*. I'll be demonstrating what an episode will be like with a cookoff, using local volunteers for the competition, and then signing autographs during the morning show at the local television studio."

"Nonsense." Ma was already shaking her head. "You Greek. You come to my Greek restaurant, *Aphrodite's*, for cookoff. I win, of course. You cook and sign autographs there. Everybody come. Okay? Okay."

"That's an interesting offer, but I won't be the one cooking in the show. I'll be judging the competing chefs and choosing one winner on each of my stops for the tour. The recipes I use in my restaurant are top secret. That's part of my uniqueness and success."

"I no peek at you ingredients. I no use recipe. That *my* success." Ma slapped her chest. "You do cookoff here and do signing, too."

Marieta studied Ma with narrowed eyes. "What's in it for you?"

Ma blinked in surprise then frowned. "You in Hollywood too long. Greek take care of Greek." She nodded. "Authentic Greek restaurant better than TV kitchen. You famous. Let camera crew come to you."

Marieta relaxed, eyeing Ma with respect. "You're right. I have been away from genuine Greek hospitality for far too long." She sighed. "It's a brutal, competitive world out there. Makes a chef grow hard." She smiled her first genuine smile. "How can I say no to such a lovely offer? I'll see if the station minds changing the location of the cookoff."

"And I cut you hair for free." Aunt Tasoula shooed me out of her chair, her hands moving in time with her words. "Kalli no mind."

I quickly stepped out of the way. "By all means, my hair can wait."

Marieta nodded her thanks to me and took my

spot as my aunt got to work, talking and snipping away.

Suddenly, Chloe burst through the doors, her face flushed and eyes red from crying. My aunt's scissors flailed wildly as she greeted us. That was the danger of letting her cut your hair when she was distracted—you either ended up injured or bald.

Marieta looked horrified and kept ducking until my aunt calmed down.

"What happened, sweetie?" Aunt Tasoula asked, concern etched on her face.

"That beast make me so angry!" Chloe plopped down into the seat beside my ma.

Ma fanned her face with the magazine she still held. "What he do? I take care of him. He never know what coming." Ma nodded fiercely, her beehive bobbing in agreement.

"He say he come back for me, but now his girlfriend, Sigrid, show up in town. He no change at all," Chloe cried.

Aunt Tasoula's eyebrows shot up in surprise. "Wait ... I thought you engaged to Cappy Quinny."

"Cappy?" Ma let out a frustrated sigh and shook her head as she continued to fan Chloe's face. "It's Captain Quincy, you nitwit."

Aunt Tasoula shrugged. "I think Cutey Cappy Quinny have nice ring to it." She winked.

Ma rolled her eyes at my aunt and turned her attention back to Chloe. "Anyway ... you still engaged?"

"Yes, no ... I don't know," Chloe wailed.

"You no like the captain?" Ma asked with concern evident in her large eyes.

"I love him," Chloe admitted.

"Then why you no marry him?" Aunt Tasoula chimed in.

"I no want to steal Nikos' thunder," Chloe said apologetically, sending a guilty glance my way.

"Oh, you don't have to worry about that," I spoke up, trying to ease her guilt and swallow my own anxiety over this. "We're in no rush. Trust me." I hesitated a moment. "If you don't mind me asking, are you still in love with Bjorn?"

"He make me so mad, but I don't know if I ever stopped loving him."

"So, you want to marry Thor's papa now?" Aunt Tasoula asked.

"I don't know what I want." Chloe sighed. "It all such a mess."

"What does Bjorn have to say about Sigrid?" I interjected, my curiosity getting the best of me.

"He say she still married to some businessman in New York City. That why he broke up with her, but she no accept it. She here to win him back."

"And what does Captain Crenshaw have to say about all of this?" I asked, softly.

"He say call him when I know what I want, but he no happy. I no want to hurt him." Chloe sniffled.

"I knew those snakes meant trouble," Aunt Tasoula muttered gravely.

Ma's eyes narrowed as she spoke fiercely, "Maybe it time we do something about it."

I had no idea what was going on, but I did know one thing ... the mamas getting involved was the last thing we needed.

～

"Wow, it's busy in here tonight," I said as Nik and I walked into *Flannigan's Pub*.

I was immediately greeted by the warm, dim

lighting and the bustling crowd of people mingling and laughing. The walls were lined with dark wood paneling and the ceilings adorned with old-fashioned chandeliers. The bar was bustling with activity, bartenders expertly mixing drinks while patrons sat on stools, chatting and sipping their beverages. Classic rock music was booming out of the speakers.

The smell of hearty pub food wafted through the air, mingling with the scent of beer and whisky. I could also catch a hint of old wood. The floors were made of weathered hardwood, worn smooth from years of foot traffic.

Michael Flannigan and his wife, Lois, owned the Irish pub. They didn't have any children, so the pub was his baby. He adored his red-headed, rosy-cheeked, cherubic wife and didn't so much as blink over her shopping obsession because it made her happy. Lois knew everything about everyone and was a regular at Jaz's boutique.

Flannigan's was a favorite of ours.

My cousins, Kosmos and Silas, who owned *Diner Delights,* were there with their girlfriends, mail carrier Winnie Wallabe and bartender Zena Renner, as well as Nik's lawyer cousin, Thalia, and her senator boyfriend, Parker West.

Jaz and Boomer flagged us over to a couple spots they saved at a table.

"Hi guys, where's Yanni?" I asked as I sat down, after I wiped off my seat with an alcohol wipe, of course.

Nik was grabbing us some drinks.

Yanni was my oldest cousin who owned a landscaping business called *Yanni's Yards.* His girlfriend, Claudett Fox, was his assistant.

"He's actually working late with Natalie and Father

Papadopoulos on a plan to redo the landscaping in hopes of helping to fix the snake infestation." Boomer took a sip of his beer. "I'm not going near that place unless all else fails."

"What place?" Nik asked as he sat down to join us and handed me a glass of Chardonnay while he sipped his whisky.

"Church," I said, wiping off the rim of my glass three times.

"Apparently, my father is now steering clear of Ma since Sigrid arrived. He's avoiding her as well, spending his time helping Natalie. He's very knowledgeable when it comes to all kinds of snakes after learning a lot from his best friend." Nik shook his head. "Snakes he can handle. Women not so much. I was really hoping to go at least a couple months without any more drama."

"Speaking of drama," Boomer interjected, "Look over at the bar. That slick dude with the bodyguards is Sigrid's wealthy bigwig business tycoon husband, Niles Turner. She claims she filed for divorce, but he won't let her. That's why she moved to Norway, but apparently, he has eyes on her at all times. Has for years."

"For someone who wants nothing to do with him, why is she sitting next to him at the bar?" I watched the blonde bombshell allow her stiff suit *ex* buy her a drink.

"Sounds like she has an M.O. when it comes to her dating life. Wealthy businessmen who can keep her in the lifestyle she's used to," Jaz pointed out.

Nik grunted. "Last I talked to my father, he told me he was on the verge of finalizing a business venture that would set him up for the rest of his life so he would have time for the more important things, like family. That was why he moved to Norway. But I haven't talked to him in a while. Suddenly, he shows up. He says he wants to move to Clearview to win Ma back and to be closer to me since I'm engaged and might give him grandchildren."

"Grandchild," I corrected. I'd only agreed to one child, and even that still terrified me.

"But I'm guessing there has to be another reason. He's never given up everything for Ma and me before," Nik went on as if he hadn't heard me.

I sighed. We sat there for a moment in silence.

"Oh, did I tell you that Father Papadopoulos has enlisted Thalia's help to get Theo Harris off his back," Nik added.

"Isn't he that land developer?" Jaz asked.

Boomer nodded. "Even though the church is ancient, it has never been designated a historic landmark. Theo has been buying up the land around the church for a big development project for years. The only thing standing in his way of finishing the deal is the church itself. He would love nothing more than a good scandal to scare the parishioners away so the church will be hurting financially, and he can swoop in for a land grab if it goes under."

"Well, the snakes and the legend have certainly made the news." I looked around the packed bar. "If Theo is behind this, his plan has clearly backfired. I've never seen so many outsiders who've flocked to Clearview to get a peek at the snakes and hear about the legend. The church is more popular than ever."

"Tourists, Kalli. Gotta love 'em. It's crazy what a little controversy can do for business," Jaz said, her eyes twinkling with amusement. "I mean, every pet psychic and snake charmer from here to New York City is probably setting up shop right now."

"That's all we need. Crazy people trying to touch the snakes for good luck. Someone's gonna get bit and sue the town, mark my words." Boomer leaned back and crossed his arms. "I don't like this one bit."

"You and me both, partner." Nik took a hefty sip of whisky and winced. "The captain is already in a bad enough mood because of my dad interfering in his relationship with Ma, even though he's seemed to have backed off. His timing couldn't be worse. Don't get me wrong, I love my father, but we get along much better when he stays international where he belongs."

"I'm glad I finally got to meet him, although I wish it were under different circumstances," I said.

"I planned to take you to Norway after I proposed," Nik shot me a pointed look, "but then you didn't let me propose because you needed a girls' trip to think, and we all know how that turned out."

"Marriage is a big step. You know how I overthink everything. That trip was necessary. It may have started off rocky with me getting accused of murder, but after my name was cleared, I proposed to you, if memory serves."

"Exactly," he muttered, "and we haven't had a moment's peace since."

I blinked. "Do you regret saying yes?"

He looked at me startled. "What? No, I—"

Just then, a loud crash echoed from the direction of the bar.

We all turned to see a group of rowdy tourists who had knocked over a half-dozen beer glasses in their excitement. The shards glinted like dangerous confetti against the hardwood floor.

Nik sighed heavily, setting his drink down with a clink before standing up. "I'm going to help Michael and save him the step of calling for backup from the police," he said, rolling his eyes as he maneuvered through the crowd.

"I've got your back, buddy." Boomer jumped up to join him.

"Good idea before they start throwing punches," Jaz said, shaking her head and sipping her Riesling. "Better for business or not, I have a feeling things are only going to get worse."

I took a sip of my Chardonnay, half-listening to my cousins go back and forth about which one of them would catch a snake first if they ventured near the church. For better or worse ... this was my life.

4

It was August fifteenth.

Jaz and I had been trying to iron out the last of the wedding details, finalizing seating charts, and going to final dress fittings. Her wedding was right around the corner ... and the snakes were still there. Father Papadopoulos decided to hold a special service for the Dormition of Virgin Mary. So much for the snakes deterring people ... the crowds had only grown.

Retired Anthropology professor, Oliver Grant, had shown up, fascinated by the legend of the snakes. He specialized in Greek mythology. He had silver-streaked, golden-blond hair and big green eyes behind even bigger spectacles. He was talking with Father and Sister, while Natalie and Bjorn were trying to stop tourists from touching the snakes, including Sigrid.

She seemed to be the worst offender.

Chloe was with the mamas in a united front, steering clear of both Bjorn and Sigrid.

Meanwhile, an investigative journalist from out of town named Samuel Brooks, with his brown man bun and small round glasses, was sticking his microphone in Nik's face. "Detective Stevens, do you believe the snake infestation is connected to any recent criminal activity in Clearview? Some locals are saying it's a sign of bad omens."

Nik chuckled, the kind of laugh that could charm even the most skeptical. "With all due respect, Mr. Brooks, if every snake was a criminal mastermind, I'd have a lot more work on my hands than I already do." He winked, but I could see the annoyance he was struggling to squash. He started walking.

"C'mon, Detective. A little serious journalism here," Samuel pressed as he kept up. "The small-town rumor mill is buzzing about potential corruption linked to the church. Maybe they staged the snakes to make the legend seem real. Do you think there's something more sinister at play?"

I leaned closer to hear what would they would say next while also keeping an eye on the scene unfolding around us. A pair of curious children had started inching toward the snakes, their parents obliviously distracted by Oliver's animated stories on Greek folklore.

"Listen, Brooks," Nik replied, his tone growing more serious and clearly losing his patience. "Before we jump to conclusions, let's remember that snakes are just snakes. There are all sorts of reasons they could suddenly appear." He glanced around, clearly trying to gauge how many people were watching.

Several eyes and ears were focused on us.

At that moment, my hands twitched in my lap, itching to grab some hand sanitizer. I could practically feel the germs in the air from all the tourists present.

"Nik," I whispered, leaning forward slightly to catch his attention as he finished up with Samuel. "What if it's not just snakes coming to the surface because of nature? What if there's some bizarre connection we're missing?"

Before I could elaborate further, squeals rang out, drawing Samuel's attention. The two children had reached the snakes and were now bouncing on their heels, pointing at one of the wriggling reptiles drawing near.

"Missing? You mean like someone deliberately brought the snakes in?" Nik raised an eyebrow, his expression shifting from annoyance to being impressed. "The though has crossed my mind. Good intuition, Ballas."

"Thanks," I said.

"However," Nik added, his voice lowering, "I think we should also be cautious about how rumors spread faster than the snakes themselves."

"Agreed," I said.

Just then, a loud, shrill scream pierced the air.

I whipped my head around to see one of the tourists—a frazzled woman with a big floppy sun hat —leap back from the snake curling around her feet like it had sprouted legs and decided to chase her. The children squealed in delight, while their parents turned to investigate the commotion.

I had the strongest sensation of being watched. I cast a quick glance around the bustling courtyard, but there were so many people, it could be anyone. I shrugged off the sensation, and my gaze landed on a woman with oversized glasses, standing off on the side by herself. I'd never seen her before. Then again, there were a lot of outsiders in town at the moment.

I leaned closer to Nik, my voice barely above a whisper. "That woman ... over there. She seems out of place. I know it sounds crazy, but I can't shake the feeling that she's here for a reason other than the snakes."

Nik followed my gaze, his brow furrowing. "Maybe she's Greek?"

"She's as blond as your father."

"Well, so are you." He shoved his hands in his pockets. "Maybe she's adopted."

"I'm not buying those odds."

He studied her closer. "She's probably just another curious onlooker?"

"Maybe," I mused, my curiosity piqued as the woman stayed to the shadows, far away from the snakes and the growing crowd.

"Alright, you stay here," Nik ordered, his tone full of command and brooking no argument. "I'll go talk to her."

As he strode off, I tried to quell the fluttering in my stomach. There was always some kind of drama unfolding in Clearview, like a never-ending three act play weaving itself into our lives.

Forget this. I hurried after him.

I weaved through the throngs of people, my heart racing as I kept my eyes locked on Nik's broad shoulders. The woman with the oversized glasses had shifted slightly, her gaze darting nervously around as if she felt the weight of scrutiny pressing down on her. There was something undeniably *off* about her.

"Hey, wait up!" I called out, pushing past a pack of tourists who were snapping photos of the two children who had now set up an unofficial snake petting zoo.

Even Bjorn and Natalie obviously had their hands full.

Nik paused and turned, his expression a mix of concern and amusement. "Kalli, I told you to stay put."

Ignoring him, I caught up to his side as we weaved through the crowd, ducking past families and their squawking children, my mind racing with questions.

What was this woman's connection to the snakes? And why did she give off that peculiar vibe?

"Hello there. Welcome to Clearview," Nik said, flashing a disarming smile that could melt even the iciest of hearts. "I couldn't help but notice you're not quite enjoying our little circus like everyone else."

Her lips tightened into a thin line, and for a moment, I could feel the brush of unease radiating off her —the kind that prickled at my fingertips. "I'm here on business, not pleasure." She glanced around with an upturned nose. "Snakes are not my thing."

"I'm Detective Stevens, and this is my fiancé, Kalli Ballas." Nik held out his hand.

"Stevens?" the woman spat, her glasses slipping down her nose, revealing the fury in her eyes before she shoved them back up.

Nik dropped his hand and stepped sightly in front of me. "You have a problem with the name Stevens?"

"You bet I do."

Nik sighed. "I take it you know my father, Bjorn Stevens?"

"*Knew* your father before he left Norway after ruining my life."

"Who are you?" Nik asked.

"Ingrid Halvorsen," Bjorn boomed from behind us, storming into the scene like Zeus himself. "What in the name of Odin are you doing here?"

"I'm here to get my money back, Bjorn Stevens, or mark my words, you'll rue the day you crossed me."

~

THE NEXT MORNING, I was in my loft at *Full Disclosure*, working on my winter line for my *Kalli Original* designs. Even though it was only August, my fall line would be coming out next week, so that meant *Interludes* would want my winter line soon.

My loft was my sanctuary.

A place where I could think and design in peace. I had mannequins of all shapes and sizes, yards of material in the most luxurious fabrics and colors, satin, lace, beads, and more to use as accents. I had a universal line for *Interludes* in New York City, but I also created commissioned designs when requested right here in Clearview.

I sketched those designs based on the women they were for. Through getting to know these women, I created items they often would never have thought to buy for themselves. It gave me such joy to watch a woman's face light up when she looked in my mirror and felt beautiful in something I made just for her.

Right now, I was working on Jaz's wedding trousseau.

"Can I come up?" Jaz called from the bottom of the stairs leading up to my loft.

It was early. She'd just opened the store, but no one had come in yet.

"Yes, they're finally ready for you to approve, and then I'll get started sewing them," I hollered down to her.

She climbed the stairs and then sanitized her hands before entering my domain with a wide smile on her face.

The moment of truth ...

"Okay, here you go. Flip through these pages and let me know what you think. I can make as many as you want, or I can start over if you're not happy. That's the beauty of sketching the designs first." I handed her my sketchbook.

Jaz perched on the edge of my worktable, her eyes

sparkling with anticipation as she flipped through the pages. I watched her expression morph from intrigue to admiration, a smile blooming as she reached the sketches for her delicate lace bralette and matching high-waisted panties.

"Oh, Kalli! These are stunning!" she exclaimed, her voice rising with enthusiasm. "You've captured exactly what I envisioned. The lace is so intricate— like it belongs in a fairytale."

I felt a surge of pride swell within me. Designing lingerie was more than just stitching fabric; it was about empowering women to embrace their beauty and feel confident in their skin. "I'm glad you like them. I thought the floral pattern would complement the country theme of your wedding perfectly."

As Jaz continued to admire my work, momentarily lost in the pages of designs, my mind wandered back to Ingrid and that ominous scene yesterday after Bjorn's looming presence had blocked out the sun.

The memory of Ingrid's fierce determination sent a shiver down my spine.

There was something undeniably menacing about her, as if she had come to Clearview with a vendetta on her mind. I couldn't shake the feeling that her presence in our quaint little town and her connection to Nik's father only added another layer of complexity to this already tangled web. They'd stormed off together to talk, leaving both Nik and I wondering what was going on. I'd filled Jaz in to get her thoughts.

"Do you think Nik should worry about Bjorn?" I pulled out some fabric samples for Jaz to look over as I talked. "I think Ingrid might be out for more than money. I think she wants revenge and might do anything to get it."

Jaz frowned, still absorbed in her admiration.

"From what you said, she did sound a bit off. I'm sure Bjorn can handle himself. He looks like a God," she replied with a teasing lilt, flipping to the last sketch, "but she is a woman who feels wronged, and we all know there's nothing scarier. But first, let's focus on these gorgeous designs! You've truly outdone yourself."

"I appreciate that," I said, following her attempt to divert the conversation back to my sketches. "But it's hard not to get sidetracked when my future family is involved. After I marry Nik, Bjorn will officially be my family, too."

Jaz set down the sketchbook, her expression shifting from admiration to concern. "Kalli, you know how families are. They come with their own set of dramas, especially a big one like Nik's. But just think of the joy of all those family gatherings. The food. The laughter. Just picture it—your ma and her famous moussaka mixed in with Bjorn's Viking stories. It's practically a sitcom waiting to happen. I can already picture the holidays, you all roasting lamb on a spit while wearing matching horned hats."

I chuckled, shaking my head. "Right? Just what I need—even more drama at the dinner table than we already have."

She burst into laughter, her joy infectious. "I'd pay good money to be at that dinner table. But seriously, I wouldn't worry too much. Nik seems to handle his family's issues pretty well. Plus, you're the queen of calm most of the time." She winked.

"Queen of calm?" I repeated, raising an eyebrow at her as I reached for a roll of lace that had unwound itself onto the floor. "Have you seen me in family gatherings? My anxiety shoots through the roof. I don't know how I survived for almost thirty years in one family like this. How am I supposed to survive adding Nik's Greek family and then a Viking side on top of that? I'm beginning to think I was meant to be single."

"It's just pre-wedding jitters." Her eyes softened and her voice gentled, "Everyone goes through it."

"I'm pretty sure everyone doesn't have families like ours." I sighed, glancing out the window where the sun was trying to break through the clouds. My thoughts circled back to Ingrid with an unsettling intensity. "I just wish I knew what Ingrid was really up to. She feels ... desperate."

"Well, you're the mind-reading fashionista; can't you just touch her and figure it out?" Jaz flashed me a devilish grin.

"Right, because nothing says, 'I'm not creepy' like touching an angry stranger just to know her motives." I rolled my eyes, trying to think of another way.

The swirling intensity of someone's innermost thoughts entering my brain took a lot out of me both physically and mentally, especially when the person's emotions ran high. I could barely deal with my own thoughts and emotions. But mind reading had proven useful to gaining answers in the past. I just had to find an excuse to touch her without freaking her out.

She wasn't exactly the warm and fuzzy type.

"I doubt I'll get close enough to try, but maybe I'll get a chance to read Bjorn. I have a feeling he can shed some light on a lot of questions we have."

"That's true, and he said he wasn't going anywhere anytime soon, so I'm sure you'll see him again?"

"Exactly!" I huffed. "I need to know what he's up to so Nik and I can get back on track. In the meantime, I need to focus on happier thoughts. Like your wedding —what's next on our agenda?"

"Next," Jaz said, flipping through my sketches once

more, "we need to discuss which one of these babies you're going to make for my wedding night because I want Boomer to think I'm a goddess."

"You already are one. I'm simply enhancing what the gods already gave you," I replied, grateful for her lighthearted distraction.

The countdown to her wedding had begun, with every passing second flying by. And then it would be my turn. I was thrilled for her and for myself, yet she'd been my best friend since we were children. Change was hard. Things were going to be different for us.

That was inevitable.

I shook off my worries and was about to look at the design Jaz had picked out, when my phone buzzed in my hand, startling me.

I shot a puzzled look at Jaz before answering the call. "Nik, what's up?" I asked, curious why he was calling when I knew he was busy.

"You won't believe what Father Papadopoulos found on the church grounds this morning," Nik said, his voice tight with unmistakable worry.

"More snakes?" I guessed, not surprised by anything that happened in our small town anymore.

"It's worse than that," he replied grimly. "He found a dead body."

Jaz looked up in surprise and covered her mouth, clearly hearing him through the phone.

My heart dropped as my eyes met hers, and I gasped in shock. "Oh my, Zeus, poor Father Papadopoulos."

"Poor Sigrid. She's the victim. The coroner said she died by a snake bite," Nik added.

Jaz looked at me confused, her thoughts obviously mirroring my own. "But I thought Natalie said these snakes aren't venomous?"

"Apparently, this one was," Nik said gravely, pausing a beat before adding, "and my father is the prime suspect."

My mind raced as I processed this information. My fiancé's father was potentially involved in a murder? The wedding suddenly felt so insignificant compared to these devastating events unfolding.

5

As I hung up the phone, the laughter and excitement of the bridal sketches faded into an echoing silence. My heart raced as I processed all the details Nik had filled me in on regarding the gravity of his news.

Sigrid was dead, and now the specter of suspicion loomed over his father like a dark cloud.

"Did I hear something about a dead body?" Jaz asked, her voice dropping an octave as she leaned in closer, her expression somber.

I nodded slowly, feeling the weight of the moment settle heavily over us. "Sigrid's dead, and they think Nik's dad might be involved."

Jaz's mouth fell open, and she clutched my sketchbook like a shield. "Oh no! Poor Nik. This is not what he needs right now."

"No kidding. Apparently, she was found in the garden this morning by the church staff with a snake bite on her," I added, shuddering at the thought. "Obviously it was poisonous, so now we have a lethal snake on the loose."

"Oh, my lord, Boomer is going to faint when he hears about this." She shuddered. "It's a good thing we're not Greek or getting married in the church. I think he would call off the wedding before facing a poisonous snake."

"I'm sure Boomer has already heard. Good thing *our* wedding isn't any time soon, but that's a problem for another day. At the moment, I'm more worried about Bjorn being the prime suspect? Nik has to be a wreck about it, but he's not letting on." I frowned. "He's not talking about his feelings much these days, period. It's really starting to get to me. Do you think he has cold feet?"

Jaz was already shaking her head. "That man is crazy about you. I think the family drama is just getting to him. Let him focus on the case, then once everything is solved, I'm sure you'll get back on track in the wedding planning department."

"I hope you're right." I sighed, making up my mind about something. "All the more reason to help solve this case. You in?"

"You know it." Jaz grinned. "Okay, so I know Sigrid was Bjorn's ex-girlfriend, but why does that make him the main suspect?"

"I guess she found out Ingrid was in town and went to see her and then she went to the church to find Bjorn, who was still helping Natalie," I explained, recalling what Nik had told me. "Father Papadopoulos insists he saw Bjorn and Sigrid arguing late last night."

"I wonder what was so important it couldn't wait until morning?" Jaz mused.

"There's talk about Sigrid having discovered something concerning Bjorn and Ingrid. Then Father thought that everyone left until this morning when his staff found Sigrid deceased in the gardens by a poisonous snake. Natalie had some confiscated ones in the back of her truck. Nik is heading to the station now to question him and asked me to be there, so I should go."

"Go ahead. I'll hold down the fort here." Jaz left my book of designs in my loft and led the way downstairs.

After gathering my things, I followed her downstairs and then headed to the police station.

TEN MINUTES LATER, I joined Nik in his office at the station for moral support. Captain Crenshaw didn't want him to work on the case because he was too close since Bjorn was his father. Boomer was in charge, but that didn't mean Nik couldn't still talk to his dad.

Bjorn looked anxious, his eyes darting around as if searching for an escape.

Nik's voice was steady and unyielding as he talked to him. "So, help me to understand, Dad. You were alone after leaving the church last night?"

"Yes. Alone all night." Bjorn nodded.

"Where did you go? Detective Matheson said the hotel cameras don't show you getting there until the wee hours of this morning."

"I drove around." Bjorn shrugged. "I needed to think about the future."

Nik paused a beat before asking, "With Ma?"

Bjorn's eyes met Nik's. "I love your mother, but I can't burden her with all this."

Nik dropped his gaze to his notebook, processing his father's words, then changed the subject. "Tell me about your relationship with Sigrid."

A flash of pain swam into Bjorn's eyes, his response hesitant, his voice firm. "We dated, but when I found out she was still married, I broke things off." His voice filled with emotion. "She refused to accept that and followed me here. Now she's dead. She didn't deserve that." He lifted his gaze to Nik's. "I didn't killer her. You believe me, don't you, son?"

"As your son, I don't know what to believe, Dad." Nik sighed, running a hand over the back of his neck. "Right now, I'm trying to be objective as a detective and just look at the facts until Detective Matheson gets here."

"Aye aye, *Detective*." Bjorn saluted Nik, his jaw muscle bulging. "I might love women a little too much, but I would never harm a single hair on any one of them. You should know me better than that."

"I *should* know you better, Dad, but I don't because you're never around." He let out a frustrated breath. "And who's fault is that?"

"That's why I came back." Bjorn's sapphire gaze so like his son's looked at him pleadingly. "To change all that."

I watched Bjorn, studying his body language and energy since I sat across the table from him and couldn't touch him to hear his thoughts. On the surface, I saw fear and guilt, but looking deeper, I caught glimpses of something darker lurking beneath Bjorn's composed facade.

Nik pressed on, his tone relentless. "You were seen arguing with Sigrid the night she died. In fact, you were the last person seen talking to her." He leaned forward. "And what is up with Ingrid, Dad? What happened between the two of you and your business venture back in Norway?"

My leg brushed Bjorn's beneath the table. His panic surged, his thoughts a chaotic whirl. *How much does he know?* My brow furrowed as he moved his leg away from mine.

Suddenly, the sound of commotion outside the

room broke the tension. I glanced over my shoulder out the window of Nik's office to see the Greek mamas entering the station with bundles of sage in their hands.

Oh, my Zeus. I got up and opened the door. The strong scent of the herb filled the air as they began waving it around, muttering incantations.

Captain Crenshaw's exasperated voice rang out as he emerged from his office. "Ladies, you can't just barge in here and—"

Chloe stepped forward; her eyes alit with determination. "We must cleanse this place of the evil spirits before anyone else is taken from us!"

"But—" he tried again.

Aunt Tasoula waved a smoking wand in front of his face. "You sit. We sage. Okay? Okay."

"Not okay—" he tried one more time.

"We save you, Quincy." Ma twirled in circles, fanning the sage until everyone was coughing.

I bit back a groan. You don't mess with Greek mamas when it comes to their beliefs. I turned my attention back to the men behind me, just in time to see Nik's steely gaze shift and Bjorn's face pale as the station door opened once more.

Following their gazes, I watched Natalie, the herpetologist, enter the room carrying a large, worn book. Her expression was grave as she approached Captain Crenshaw. "I have crucial information about the snake species involved in Sigrid's death."

"Please tell me you caught the snake." The captain scrubbed a hand through his salt and pepper hair. "The mayor is in a panic with a poisonous snake on the loose."

My interest piqued, and I watched closely.

Natalie opened the book, revealing detailed illustrations and descriptions of various snakes. "We haven't caught the snake yet, but we were able to test the venom found in Sigrid's body, so we know what we're looking for. It wasn't one of the ones I confiscated in my truck, so it was brought in from somewhere else. It matches that of a rare species known as the Atheris hispida. It's not native to this region and is highly venomous."

"Great. That doesn't ease my mind one bit." The captain let out a heavy sigh.

Nik stepped out of his office to join me, his curiosity evident. "A poisonous snake? How did it end up here in Clearview?"

Natalie nodded. "Now, that's the question, isn't it, Detective? Whoever brought this snake here knew what they were doing and did so with a clear intent."

"Murder," I whispered, feeling a sense of dread settle over me.

But who ... and why?

~

JAZ and I took our lunch break together like we tended to do these days and brought Willow and Armani to *Clearview Park* to give our other pets a break from the puppies. Not to mention, it kept them socialized.

The park was lush and green, with perfectly trimmed grass and blooming flowers of all colors. Large oak and maple trees provided ample shade and a picturesque backdrop to the park's amenities: a playground filled with giggling children, picnic tables occupied by families enjoying meals, a fenced-in dog park, a gazebo and stage for entertainment, and a small pond with ducks gliding across the surface.

The rest of the park was roped off as venders for food and games were setting up their tents for the fair, which would start in a couple of days. The midway crews were constructing and inspecting every ride. And the stage was being prepared for the lineup of entertainers.

I spotted Emily Nguyen just outside the roped off area. She was staging poses and videos with various spectators, squealing for the camera as they looked for the venomous snake, then posting the videos for her social media fans.

Oliver waited patiently at a nearby table until she was ready. I heard him telling someone he was only too happy to sit for an interview with her regarding her travel blog about the snakes. No doubt she was emphasizing the murder.

None of this was good for the fair.

I shook my head and looked at Jaz. She grabbed a burger and fries from *Fender's Food Truck* and sat at a picnic table. I joined her, after wiping down the picnic table bench, of course, then unpacked my sanitized bag of green goddess salad and iced tea.

Meanwhile, the puppies played in the outdoor pen to get socialized with other people and dogs. The trainer was working on leash training and reactivity today as well. Willow was being a little lady like her poodle mama, and Armani was being, well ... Armani —his inner Wolfgang emerging.

Captain Quincy had ordered the mamas to go home and Bjorn not to leave town. Then he'd called a meeting with Nik and Boomer to go over their suspect list.

I wasn't invited, but that didn't mean I would sit idly by.

Nik would never agree to set a wedding date if he

was worrying about his father, so I planned to go over my own list of suspects with my partner-in-crime, Jaz, and do a little investigating of my own.

In between wedding planning for her, of course.

"Okay, so Bjorn is the main suspect because he was heard arguing with Sigrid the night before she died, right?" Jaz bit into her hamburger, waiting for my reply.

"Correct. Sigrid met with Ingrid Halvorsen, Bjorn's ex-business partner, because she was jealous. Bjorn says his relationship with Ingrid was purely professional, but there was something about their business deal that wasn't on the up and up, and Bjorn's not talking." I dabbed my mouth with a napkin. "He's definitely hiding something. I heard his thoughts when our legs touched in Nik's office."

"Wow, okay." Jaz took a sip of her soda. "That's a start."

I nodded, taking a bite of my salad. "But we need more."

"If Sigrid found something out about their business, do you think either Ingrid or Bjorn could have killed Sigrid to keep her quiet?" Jaz asked.

"Nik says his father is a lot of things, but not a killer. I don't know anything about Ingrid, though, and she did seem furious when she came to town. She could have killed her out of revenge to get back at Bjorn." I sipped my tea.

"Speaking of romance, what about Sigrid's husband, Niles Turner?" Jaz wrote in her notebook as she popped a French fry in her mouth.

"Bjorn claims he didn't know Sigrid was married. She'd said she filed for divorce, but Niles wouldn't sign the papers. That was why she moved back to her homeland, but he has kept tabs on her all along.

Once she came back to the states, he tracked her down."

"Niles could have killed her in a crime of passion. You know, like if he can't have her, then no one can." Jaz made a note.

"True. He's from the city and has some questionable colleagues who look like snakes themselves."

"I can only imagine. Niles doesn't seem like someone you want to be on the bad side of." Jaz finished her burger and took a sip of soda.

I nodded. "On another note, even though the legend takes place in Greece, people think the sheer number of snakes on August fifteenth is no coincidence. They think by some miraculous occurrence the legend is now happening in Clearview. So much for the snakes bringing good luck by touching them. Sigrid died touching a snake, hoping for good luck to win Bjorn back."

"That's crazy. Speaking of legends and snakes. What about a local angle for more suspects." Jaz tapped her pencil. "I know the historical society has been trying to declare the church a historic landmark with Evangeline Marinakis taking the lead, but it hasn't happened yet. She is obsessed with preserving the legacy of the church. I heard Evangeline wasn't too happy about people swarming all over sacred grounds, trying to touch the snakes. She would do anything to keep people away. Maybe she was trying to scare Sigrid away by planting a poisonous snake to hurt her but it ended up killing her."

"Possibly, and then there's Theo Harris the land developer. I wouldn't put it past him to plant a poisonous snake. Sigrid's death proves there's no good luck from touching the snakes, only the trouble the parishioners feared. He might be trying to scare the members into leaving the church so it will go under before it's declared a historic landmark so he can swoop in for a land grab. Nik said the church is having financial problems already and wouldn't survive a mass exodus."

Jaz handed me her notebook. "I think that's a pretty good list of suspects to look into to start with."

Barking erupted and people started shouting. I looked over to the dog pen and gaped, while Jaz gasped. Armani led the pack, charging in our direction, with Willow hot on his heels and all the other dogs loose, running helter-skelter. The trainer was running around in circles, grabbing at leashes to no avail.

"Oh no," I said, quickly gathering my things and throwing my trash out. "That's our cue. Lunch is officially over."

Jaz was already on her feet with a look that could freeze a volcano. "And one puppy is officially in the doghouse."

We quickly made our way over to the madhouse, trying to catch any of the dogs before they could escape onto the busy streets outside of the park. Luckily, some of the volunteers had noticed as well and were helping us corral the dogs back into their pen.

"Who let them out?" Jaz asked sternly as we struggled to round up a particularly squirmy terrier.

"I-I'm not sure," one volunteer stuttered nervously. "I turned away for just a moment to grab some treats for them, and when I looked back they were all out."

Jaz sighed in frustration but didn't have time for further scolding as we still had several dogs to catch. We finally managed to wrangle all of them back into their pen, except for Armani who was still running around excitedly.

"Come here boy," Jaz called out, holding out her hand for him to sniff.

But Armani wasn't interested in coming back just yet. He was having too much fun racing around and causing mischief with Willow.

I shook my head at him fondly, seeing so much of Wolfgang, before turning towards Willow. She was looking more than a little sheepish now that she knew she was in trouble. She sat like a prim and proper lady, waiting for my next command.

"Oh, so now you act like a well-mannered, perfectly trained little missy. I'm onto you," I said sternly, but couldn't help grinning at her adorable face.

Finally, managing to get both dogs back into their respective pens, Jaz and I let out a sigh of relief.

"Well, that was quite the adventure," Jaz said.

"Or was it ...?" I mused.

Jaz frowned. "What do you mean?"

I shrugged. "I'm not sure. Did someone walk by and hear what we were talking about?"

"You think that maybe someone was trying to send us a warning?" Jaz's eyes widened as if just now realizing we could be in danger.

My eyes narrowed. "I think maybe it's time we made things perfectly clear. We're on the case and not going to stop following clues until it's solved."

6

Sunday brunch after the Divine liturgy service at our Greek orthodox church rotated between the Ballas family and the Pagonis family. It was Nik's ma, Chloe's, turn, but she was under stress since Bjorn had changed his mind on reconciling and Quincy wasn't sure if he wanted to marry her anymore, so, this week was being held at Ma and Pop's house.

The mamas were all abuzz about how many people had signed up for the *Hades' Kitchen* cookoff, especially Vincenzo Ricci—owner of *Vincenzo's* Italian restaurant and Ma's arch nemesis. Marietta didn't discriminate, meaning you didn't have to be Greek to cook Greek food, much to Ma's dismay.

Marieta had a chain of *Hades' Kitchen* restaurants across the U.S., and the winner of each episode won a substantial cash prize and the chance to work as a chef in a restaurant of Marietta's choosing.

Since this wasn't a real episode and just a single day demonstration of the show, the contestants would be narrowed down to two finalists who would do a cookoff of a Greek dish and Marietta would choose the winner. A smaller cash prize and bragging rights would be the reward, followed by an autograph signing with the audience. She would go around sampling various entrees from each chef to choose the finalists.

Ma was really only worried about Vinny as her competition.

Nik and Boomer sat with Jaz and me, filling us in on how the investigation was going. They had chosen to look into Theo Harris first. Now that the murder had happened, fewer tourists were coming around, so Theo was pressuring the diocese to sell. They weren't a landmark, and they were hurting financially. He was even offering a relocation package. Father Papadopoulos was fighting the offer, trying to convince the diocese that Holy Trinity was worth saving.

As the conversation continued, I found my gaze drifting across the yard. The warm August sun filtered through the leaves of the old oak trees, casting dappled shadows across the picnic tables. The air was filled with the aroma of grilled meats and freshly baked pastries, mingling with the laughter and chatter of our extended family.

My eyes landed on Bjorn, who was sitting at a table with Chloe and Captain Crenshaw. The tension among the three of them was palpable even from a distance. Bjorn's usual jovial demeanor seemed subdued, his broad shoulders hunched as if carrying an invisible weight. Chloe kept glancing between the two men, her expression a mix of concern and conflict. My heart went out to her, but I didn't know how to help.

"Earth to Kalli," Jaz's voice broke through my reverie.

"Sorry, you were saying?"

"Just that, thankfully, Nik's cousin Thalia is a great

lawyer. Hopefully, she'll be able to help keep the church open."

"Speak of the devil. I was hoping I would see you today," Nik said as Thalia approached our table.

She flashed a warm smile as she joined us, her dark curls bouncing as she sat down. "I wouldn't miss Ophelia's spanakopita for the world. Or risk Aunt Chloe's wrath." She laughed. "Seriously, though. How's the investigation going?"

Nik sighed, running a hand through his hair. "Slow. We've been looking into Theo Harris, but so far nothing concrete. How are things on your end?"

"Well, I've been doing some digging into the church's property records," Thalia replied, her voice dropping to a conspiratorial whisper. "It turns out there's an old clause in the deed that could complicate things if the church were to close or be sold."

I leaned in, intrigued. "What kind of clause?"

Thalia's eyes sparkled with the thrill of legal intrigue. "Apparently, if the church ever ceases to operate as a place of worship, the land reverts back to the descendants of the original donor. And get this ... the donor wasn't Greek."

Jaz gasped dramatically. "Interesting."

"Exactly." Thalia nodded. "The original donor was a wealthy English merchant who had ties to the area back in the late 1800s. His name was Reginald Blackheart."

"Blackheart?" I repeated, the name not ringing any bells.

Nik's eyes narrowed in concentration. "The Blackheart descendants could be anyone in town. Maybe they know about the clause."

"We need to do some digging," Boomer chimed in,

leaning back in his chair. "I find it hard to believe no one ever knew about this clause."

"It somehow got overlooked through all the passages of each priest who has presided over *Holy Trinity*. It's a very old church," Thalia said, pausing a moment before adding, "If the church were to close due to this scandal, technically any Blackheart descendant could have a claim to the land."

I felt a chill run down my spine despite the warm day. "So now we have another potential suspect with motive. But we don't even know who they are? Do they know about the clause? Why would they even want the land?"

"All good questions we need answers to," Nik said, his detective mode fully activated. "Boomer and I will look into the Blackheart's background and see if we can uncover any leads to descendants and any financial motives or connections to developers like Theo Harris." He looked at Boomer who nodded his agreement.

"I can help with the legal angle," Thalia offered. "I'll dig deeper into the clause and see if there are any loopholes or challenges we could mount if it comes down to it."

"Good idea." I nodded. "Meanwhile, Jaz and I can try to ask around, maybe strike up some casual conversations and see if any of the old timers know anything."

"Just be careful, Ballas," Nik warned, his protective instincts flaring. "I don't need anyone else to worry about, and we don't know for sure if there are even any descendants around. But if there are, they could be dangerous."

I was about to reassure Nik when a commotion near the food table caught our attention. We all turned to see Ma frantically waving her arms and shouting in rapid-fire Greek. That was never a good sign.

"Opa! Everyone, stop eating! Stop eating right now!" she yelled, her face flushed with panic.

The day Ma wanted people to *stop* eating had to be serious.

Pop hurried over to her, trying to calm her down. "Ophelia, what's wrong?"

"The food! Something's wrong with the food!" she cried, pointing at the spread on the table. "Big snake go slip and slide by my dishes just now!"

"Are you sure? Maybe the menopause put a big pause on you brain." He felt Ma's forehead.

"I gonna pause you *pea* brain." Ma swatted his hand away.

"Ah, that happen to Cousin Alexandra." Aunt Tasoula tsked. "She never form complete thought again. Sound like skipping record." She shook her head and made the sign of the cross. "Make me dizzy."

"You brain dizzy." Ma rolled her eyes at her sister then glared at Pop. "I know snake when I see one, Amos!"

"Okay, okay." He held up his hands and backed away.

A collective gasp rippled through the crowd as people began to back away from the food table. Panic started to set in as guests looked down at their plates in horror.

Frona bounced on her pogo stick singing, "One snakey, two snakey, three snakey, four ... five snakey, six snakey, seven snakey more," with Yiayia chasing her every step of the way.

Nik and Boomer were on their feet in an instant,

rushing over to investigate. I followed close behind, my heart racing.

As we approached, I saw something long and dark slithering between the dishes of moussaka and spanakopita. My breath caught in my throat. Could it be the venomous snake that had killed Sigrid?

"Everyone, remain calm," Nik's authoritative voice cut through the noise. "Let's not jump to conclusions. Boomer, check the area."

"I'll call animal control. *You* check the area." Boomer backed far away from the table, his eyes darting everywhere at once.

As Nik moved closer to the food table, I noticed Bjorn slip away from his picnic table with Chloe and Captain Crenshaw during the distraction. His furtive glances around the yard set off alarm bells in my head.

"Jaz," I whispered urgently. "Cover for me. I'm going to follow Bjorn."

She nodded in understanding as I quietly made my exit, trailing Bjorn as he made his way towards the side of the house. I watched as he pulled out his phone and dialed a number, speaking in hushed tones.

"Hey, the snakes are here. This is getting crazy. I don't know how much longer I can keep quiet." His head whipped around, and I ducked behind a bush. He frowned. "I gotta run. Talk later." He hung up and headed back to the yard.

I stayed behind the bush.

I wanted to believe that Nik's father could be innocent, but he kept doing things like this that made him look suspicious. The question was who was he talking to ... and what did he have to be quiet about?

THE NEXT MORNING, Jaz and I stopped into *Sinfully Delicious*, the bakery owned by Maria Danza right across the street from *Full Disclosure*. Maria and Jaz used to be enemies because they both liked a carpenter named Johnny. After realizing he wasn't worth it, they both moved on and were happily engaged.

Sinfully Delicious is a cozy, quaint storefront with brightly painted walls in shades of pastel blue and pink. A vintage sign with the bakery's name in retro font hung above the door, surrounded by strands of twinkling outdoor lights.

The air was thick with the scent of freshly baked pastries and bread, mingling with the aroma of rich, freshly brewed coffee. The sweet and buttery smell of croissants and danishes had Jaz salivating. I, on the other hand, couldn't get past what those ingredients could be doing to my insides, so I always chose organic, sugar free options and herbal teas.

We placed our order to go and waited.

"Hey, isn't that Sigrid's husband, Niles, talking with Theo?" Jaz pointed to a table in the far corner.

I followed Jaz's gaze to the corner table where Niles Turner and Theo Harris were engaged in an intense conversation. Niles, with his slicked-back hair and expensive suit, looked out of place in our quaint bakery. Theo, on the other hand, seemed right at home, his weathered hands wrapped around a coffee mug as he leaned in close to Niles. Whatever they were discussing looked serious.

"Good eye," I whispered to Jaz. "Let's try to get closer without being obvious."

We casually moved to a nearby table, pretending to be engrossed in conversation while straining to hear snippets of their discussion.

"... the land is practically mine already," Theo was

saying, a smug grin on his face. "Once this snake business blows over, the church won't stand a chance, and the diocese will come to their senses."

Niles nodded, his expression unreadable. "And what about our ... other arrangement?"

Theo's voice dropped even lower. "Don't worry. Once I have the land, you'll get your cut. Just make sure you keep up your end of the bargain."

Just then, Maria approached with our order. "Here you go, ladies. One sugar-free blueberry muffin and herbal tea for Kalli, and a chocolate croissant and latte for a girl after my own heart, Ms. Jaz."

"Thanks, Maria," I said, taking the items carefully. As we turned to leave, I noticed Niles and Theo abruptly end their conversation, eyeing us suspiciously.

Once outside, Jaz and I exchanged meaningful glances. "Did you hear that?" she whispered excitedly. "Sounds like Niles and Theo are in cahoots about something related to the church land."

I nodded, my mind racing. "And it seems like Niles has some kind of 'bargain' to uphold. We need to tell Nik about this."

"Agreed. But first, we have work." Jaz led the way across the street.

Lois Flannigan was first in line, waiting patiently for Jaz to open up. "Today's the day, right?"

Jaz smiled as she unlocked her boutique and turned her sign on. "It sure is. Fifty percent off everything. My annual 'Mustgo Madness Sale!' Everything must go before I put out the back to school and work fall collection."

"Your sale is always better than Vixen's, but you didn't hear that from me." Lois giggled as she charged through the door to get to the racks first.

Jaz and I laughed as we followed her inside. Winnie and Zena arrived together moments later, followed by the mamas.

"Wow, the gang's all here," I said.

Winnie and Zena were dating my cousins, Kosmos and Silas. They'd become part of our close friend group. The only one missing was Thalia, but Nik was keeping her busy with the case.

"Of course, we here," Ma said, smoothing down her polyester pant suit. "We need clothes to wear to Jaz barn wedding."

"What do one wear to a *barn* wedding?" Aunt Tasoula asked, thumbing through the racks. "A scarecrow outfit?"

"Ohhh, and I be tinwoman. I look good in silver." Chloe patted her sleek black hair with the silver highlights she'd had Aunt Tasoula put in.

I rolled my eyes. "I'm sure Jaz has plenty of elegant options that would be perfect for a rustic chic wedding, no cowbells, straw, or tin needed. Why don't you browse around and see what catches your eye?"

As the mamas scattered to peruse the racks, I turned to Jaz. "I'm going to head up to my loft and work on some designs. Let me know if you need any help down here."

"Will do," Jaz replied, already busy assisting Lois with an armful of dresses.

I made my way up to my sanctuary, grateful for the quiet space to think. As I settled in at my drafting table, my mind wandered back to the conversation we'd overheard between Niles and Theo. What kind of bargain were they referring to? And how did it tie into the church land and Sigrid's death?

I picked up my sketchpad and began to absently draw, letting my thoughts flow. Before I knew it, I had sketched out an intricate web of connections between all the players in this mystery—Bjorn, Ingrid, Sigrid, Niles, Theo, Evangeline, Blackheart descendants ...

There were still so many missing pieces to the puzzle. I stared at my sketch, hoping for some sudden insight, when a knock at the top of the stairs startled me.

"Come in," I called out, quickly flipping my sketchpad closed.

Jaz poked her head around the corner. "Hey, sorry to bother you, but there's someone here asking for you. Says it's important."

I frowned, not expecting any visitors. "Who is it?"

"That investigative journalist, Samuel Brooks." She shrugged. "He seems pretty eager to talk to you."

My curiosity won, so I nodded. "Okay, send him up." I pushed down my anxiety, adding, "But stay close, just in case."

Moments later, Samuel appeared at the top of the stairs. He gave three pumps from my hand sanitizer station, rubbing it in good over his hands—thank you, Jaz, for instructing him. He looked at me in question, and I nodded my approval. He entered my loft with gusto, his eager eyes taking in every detail of my workspace.

"Ms. Ballas, thank you for seeing me on such short notice."

"What can I do for you, Mr. Brooks?" I asked, gesturing for him to take a seat on the settee.

He sat down, leaning forward intently. "I understand you're quite close to the investigation into Sigrid Turner's death. I was hoping you might have some insights you'd be willing to share."

I raised an eyebrow. "And why would I share any insights with you? I'm not involved in the official investigation."

Samuel leaned forward, his eyes gleaming with excitement. "Because, Ms. Ballas, I believe I have information that could blow this case wide open. Information about Bjorn Stevens and his suspicious transactions and connections."

My heart skipped a beat, but I kept my face neutral. Nik had found out that his latest big luxury resort venture with Ingrid had gone south, and a lot of people had lost a ton of money, but I didn't hear about anything illegal. Also, why did Samuel care?

"That's quite an accusation, Mr. Brooks. Do you have any proof?"

He reached into his messenger bag and pulled out a thick folder. "I've been tracking Bjorn and Ingrid's business dealings for years. There's a pattern of suspicious transactions and connections. Only someone with nefarious connections could smuggle a rare venomous snake into Clearview ..."

I held up a hand to stop him. He'd been tracking my future father-in-law for years? Who was this guy? "I'm going to have to ask you to take this information to the police. I can't be involved in spreading unsubstantiated rumors."

Samuel's face fell slightly, but he nodded. "I understand. But I want you to know that I'm not just after a sensational story. I genuinely believe there's something sinister going on here, and I want to uncover the truth. That's all I've ever wanted."

I studied him carefully, trying to gauge his sincerity. For all I knew, he could be the one with nefarious connections. Anything to get the scoop. His big break.

"I appreciate your dedication to the truth, Mr. Brooks. But you have to understand my position. Bjorn is my future father-in-law. I can't—nor do I want to—engage in speculation about his potential involvement in criminal activities."

Samuel leaned back, a thoughtful expression crossing his face. "Of course, I understand your reluctance." He pushed his glasses back up his nose. "But consider this ... what if your silence allows a dangerous criminal enterprise to continue operating? Wouldn't you want to know the truth, even if it's difficult?"

His words hit close to home, stirring up the conflicting emotions I'd been grappling with since this whole ordeal began. I loved Nik, but I couldn't stand in the way of justice. I took a deep breath, choosing my next words carefully.

"Mr. Brooks, I'm not dismissing your concerns. But I need to handle this delicately. If you have concrete evidence, I urge you to take it directly to Detective Stevens, Detective Matthews, or Captain Crenshaw. They're the ones who are authorized to investigate these claims."

While I did a little unauthorized investigating of my own.

Samuel nodded slowly, tucking the folder back into his messenger bag. "I understand. I'll do that. But Ms. Ballas, if you change your mind or come across any information you think might be relevant, please don't hesitate to contact me." He stood and handed me his business card.

I took it reluctantly. "I'll keep that in mind, Mr. Brooks. Thank you for bringing this to my attention."

As Samuel stood to leave, a thought struck me. "Before you go, may I ask ... how did you come across this information?"

He paused at the top of the stairs, a cryptic smile

playing on his lips. "Let's just say I have my sources. Good day, Ms. Ballas."

After he left, I sat back in my chair, my mind reeling from this new development. Could Bjorn really be involved in something dangerous and illegal? And if so, how did it connect to Sigrid's death?

I picked up my sketchpad again, adding Samuel Brooks and his allegations to my web of connections. The picture was getting more complex by the minute.

7

At lunchtime, Jaz and I headed to *Diner Delights*, my cousins' authentic Greek diner. The diner was a feast for the senses, with the aroma of lemon and garlic hanging thick in the air, the clatter of dishes and the hum of conversation filling the space, and bright blue and white decor that evoked the spirit of the Mediterranean.

Silas stood behind the cash register, tall with curly black hair and dimples. He'd always been the biggest charmer in town until he met his match in Zena.

Then there was Kosmos. He made the food. Short and built like a tank with dark hair cropped tight. Tough as nails, but his soft sleepy bedroom eyes gave him away. Winnie was a tall voluptuous Amazon queen, and he'd been a goner as soon as he'd laid eyes on her.

"There's our Kalliope and her sidekick, Jivin' Jazlyn." Silas grinned. "Up to trouble, no doubt."

"You know it." Jaz grinned back.

They were two peas in a pod.

I rolled my eyes. "*You* should know all about trouble."

"Not these days. I'm a changed man." He held up his hands. "Compliments of one Ms. Zena Renner."

Jaz pointed at him. "Bless her heart. I wonder if she knows what she's getting into dating the likes of you."

"About the same as your detectives know what they're getting into marrying you both." He laughed. "At least we keep life interesting."

"Ignore this delinquent. How's Nik doing with his father being a suspect in the murder case?" Kosmos asked from behind the sandwich station.

I sighed and lifted my hands. "He's determined to get to the truth, but I can tell the thought that his father might be involved at all really bothers him. They're not close, but it's still his Pop."

"That's why we will do all we can to help. What Boomer and Nik don't know won't hurt them, as long as it leads to solving the case." Jaz nodded once. "Four heads are better than two, and all that."

"Until two of those heads land themselves in trouble." Silas grunted.

"Just be careful, ladies," Kosmos said. "Now what can we get you?"

"I'll have the Greek salad with grilled chicken, dressing on the side," I said. "And a sparkling water with lemon, please."

"And I'll take the gyro platter with extra tzatziki," Jaz added. "Oh, and a Diet Coke. Gotta save room for dessert." She winked.

"Coming right up," Kosmos said, turning to prepare our orders.

As we waited, I noticed the church maintenance man, Cole, and the groundskeeper, Dale, having lunch together. That wasn't unusual, but when Evangeline Marinakis came storming in and headed in their direction, I knew it wasn't going to be good. She started arguing with them about how the entire church staff was letting everyone make a mockery of the church, and it wasn't right.

As Evangeline's voice rose, Cole and Dale looked increasingly uncomfortable. I nudged Jaz and we subtly moved closer to hear better.

"You two should be ashamed of yourselves!" Evangeline hissed. "Letting all these tourists trample over sacred ground, trying to touch the snakes like it's some kind of petting zoo. Don't you care about preserving our history?"

Dale held up his hands defensively. "Now, Ms. Marinakis, we're just doing our jobs. Father Papadopoulos said—"

"Father Papadopoulos doesn't understand the gravity of the situation," Evangeline cut him off. "This isn't just about tourism or publicity. It's about respecting our traditions and keeping our church alive."

Cole sighed heavily. "Look, we get it. But with everything that's happened—the murder, the investigation—our hands are tied. We can't just start chasing people away. We have all we can do just to maintain the grounds."

Evangeline's eyes flashed dangerously. "Well, someone needs to do something before it's too late or there won't be anything to maintain. Mark my words, if we don't put a stop to this disrespect, there will be consequences."

Evangeline's ominous words hung in the air as she stormed out of the diner, the bell above the door jingling angrily in her wake.

Cole and Dale exchanged worried glances before returning to their meals, their appetites seemingly diminished.

Jaz and I shared a meaningful look. "Sounds like Evangeline is pretty worked up about this whole snake situation," Jaz whispered.

I nodded, my mind racing. "Yeah, and that bit about 'consequences' sounded almost like a threat. Do you think she could be involved somehow?"

Before Jaz could respond, Silas appeared with our food. We headed back to our table.

"Here you go, ladies. One Greek salad with grilled chicken, dressing on the side, and one gyro platter with extra tzatziki." He set the plates down in front of us. "Oh, and I couldn't help but overhear ... Evangeline's always been passionate about the church's history, but I've never seen her this riled up before."

"It does seem pretty extreme," I agreed, carefully arranging my napkin. "I wonder if there's more to her concerns than just preserving tradition."

Jaz nodded thoughtfully as she bit into her gyro. "Maybe we should do some digging into Evangeline's background. See if she has any connections to the church land or the Blackheart family."

"Good idea," I said, spearing a piece of chicken with my fork.

As we ate, I couldn't shake the feeling that we were missing something crucial. The pieces of the puzzle were there, but they weren't quite fitting together yet.

Suddenly, the bell above the door jingled as Cole and Dale left. A movement from the corner of the diner caught my eye. Oliver Grant, the retired Anthropology professor, stood up and made his way over to us.

"Ms. Ballas, Ms. Alvarez, it's nice to see you both." He greeted us with a nod. "Mind if I join you for a moment?"

I gestured to the empty chair at our table. "Not at all, Professor Grant. Please, have a seat."

Oliver settled into the chair, his eyes twinkling behind his spectacles. "I couldn't help but overhear Ms. Evangeline's impassioned conversation about the church and the snake legend. I think I might have some information that could be of interest to you both."

"Why do you think we would need information?" I said nonchalantly. "Our detectives are the investigators."

He smiled wisely. "In my experience, behind every good man is one damn clever woman." He cleared his throat. "Pardon my French."

"I like him." Jaz laughed, then we exchanged a quick glance before turning our attention back to Oliver.

"What kind of information?" I asked, trying to keep my tone casual.

Oliver leaned in, lowering his voice. "Well, in my research on local legends and mythology, I've come across some rather fascinating connections between the church's history and certain ... shall we say, less savory elements of Clearview's past."

My interest was sparked. "What do you mean by 'less savory elements'?"

"Smuggling, primarily," Oliver replied, his eyes darting around as if checking for eavesdroppers. "Back in the late 1800s and early 1900s, there were rumors of an underground network using the church as a front for their operations. Exotic animals, artifacts, you name it. It was the perfect cover."

Jaz's eyebrows shot up. "And you think this might be connected to what's happening now?"

Oliver nodded enthusiastically. "It's certainly possible. History has a way of repeating itself, after all. And with the recent appearance of that rare venomous snake ... well, it does make one wonder."

I stared at him, fascinated. "Do you have any evidence of this smuggling network? Or is it just local legend?"

"Ah, that's the tricky part," Oliver said, adjusting his glasses. "Most of it is hearsay and old stories passed down through generations. I'm afraid most of it is circumstantial. Old newspaper clippings, diary entries. But I did come across some interesting documents in the town archives: shipping manifests, cryptic letters, that sort of thing. Nothing conclusive, mind you, but enough to raise suspicions."

I felt a chill run down my spine despite the warm temperature in the diner. "That's quite a theory, Professor. But how would this connect to the current situation?" I studied him closely. "And to Sigrid's murder?"

"Ah, that's the million-dollar question, isn't it?" Oliver's eyes glittered with excitement. "I don't have all the answers, but I do know this—legends often have a kernel of truth at their core. And sometimes, the past has a way of resurfacing when we least expect it." He tapped the table twice.

Jaz tilted her head, her food forgotten. "Do you have any documents or records with you now?"

Oliver's expression turned apologetic. "Everything is back at my hotel, I'm afraid. I've been compiling it all for a book I'm writing on small-town local legends. The snakes drew me to Clearview. I'd be happy to share my research with you both, if you're interested."

"Absolutely." I exchanged contact information with him. "Thank you, professor. You've been most helpful."

"And you'll be most clever, I'm sure." He gave me a knowing nod and then left without another word.

~

LATER THAT NIGHT, Nik and I were at home in our newly remodeled house with Wolfgang, Willow, and Prissy. I'd changed into yoga pants, a tank top, and bare feet. While he wore nylon shorts, a t-shirt, and bare feet as well.

We'd finished feeding the pets, having our own dinner, and doing the dishes. Now we were sitting on our back deck, having wine and whiskey in the balmy evening air as we compared notes and talked about our day. The dogs played in the fenced-in yard and Miss Priss perched on the railing, watching the birds and squirrels.

Nik took a sip of his whiskey, his brow furrowed in thought. "So, Oliver Grant thinks there might be a connection between the current situation and some old smuggling network from over a century ago?"

I nodded, swirling my wine glass. "It seems far-fetched, I know. But with that rare venomous snake showing up out of nowhere, it does make you wonder."

"It's an interesting theory," Nik admitted. "But without concrete evidence, it's hard to pursue. We need something more tangible to go on."

"What about Niles and Theo's conversation that Jaz and I overheard?" I asked. "That seemed pretty suspicious."

Nik nodded, swirling the amber liquid in his glass. "Tell me more about that."

I recounted the snippets of conversation we'd overheard at the bakery, watching as Nik's expression grew more serious with each detail.

"That definitely sounds like something worth looking into," he said, typing a note into his phone. "I'll ask Detective Stone to talk to his New York City colleagues and see if he can find any more information on what connections Niles Turner actually has, and how he might be connected to Theo."

"And what about Evangeline?" I asked.

Nik sighed, running a hand through his hair.

"Evangeline is definitely passionate about preserving the church's history, but I'm not sure if that passion extends to murder. Still, we can't rule anyone out at this point." He took a sip of whiskey, watching the dogs play.

I nodded, taking a sip of my wine. "What about your father? Have you made any progress there?"

Nik's expression darkened slightly. "Pop's still not being entirely forthcoming. I know he's hiding something, but I can't figure out what. And without concrete evidence, I can't push too hard without compromising the investigation."

I reached out and placed my hand on his arm, feeling the tension in his muscles. "I'm sorry, Nik. I know this must be incredibly difficult for you."

He covered my hand with his, giving it a gentle squeeze. *Thanks, babe.*

I winked as a response to his thoughts and blew him a kiss.

He smiled, then his smile faded as a sigh escaped his lips. "I just wish I knew what he was mixed up in. And why he won't trust me enough to tell me the truth."

We sat in silence for a moment, the only sounds were the gentle breeze rustling through the trees and the distant barking of Wolfgang and Willow as they chased each other around the yard.

"Oh, I almost forgot to tell you," I said, suddenly remembering something. I paused a minute, unsure of how he might react. "That investigative journalist, Samuel Brooks, came to see me at my loft today."

Nik's eyebrows shot up. "Brooks? What did he want?"

I recounted my conversation with Samuel, watching as Nik's expression grew more troubled.

"He claims to have evidence of suspicious transactions involving your father and Ingrid over the years, but especially with their latest venture," I finished. "I told him to take it to you or Boomer or Captain Crenshaw directly."

Nik nodded slowly, his jaw clenching. "Good call. I'll look into it, but Brooks seems like he's more interested in sensationalism than facts. We'll have to tread carefully there." He shook his head. "Dad's had a few questionable business decisions in the past, but I guess this latest luxury resort didn't just fail. It ruined many people. I'm not sure of everything that went down, but I'm pretty sure that's why he came to Clearview to hide out while the dust settles."

"What's our next move?" I asked.

Nik took another sip of his whiskey before carefully answering. "*I* keep digging, Ballas. I'll follow up on the Niles and Theo angle and see what I can find out about this supposed evidence Brooks has. In the meantime, *you* just be there for me, okay?" He kissed me softly. "Please?" He kissed me again. *I can't bear the thought of losing you.*

I squeezed his hand, wanting to reassure him. "I promise I ..." I looked out at the yard and gasped. "Wolfgang, stop digging!" I looked at Nik with exasperation. "He's teaching Willow naughty behaviors and ruining my garden."

"Don't worry, I've got them." Nik let out a sharp whistle and jogged down the steps to bring the dogs in.

I let out a sigh of relief. I didn't want to add to his worry, but I had no intention of stopping my investigation ...

I would just have to be a little more *clever*.

8

Today was the day that Marieta was announcing the finalists at *Aphrodite's* for the *Hades' Kitchen* cookoff. She'd finished tasting all the competitor's entrees and had narrowed down the contestants to two chefs.

Everyone was there as Marieta Galanis was kind of a big deal: Marieta and her security detail, all the mamas, Jasper and the rest of *Aphrodite's* employees, of course. Plus, the regulars, the mayor, visitors in town for the upcoming fair and to see the snakes, as well as Vincenzo himself—who swore he'd never step foot in *Aphrodite's* again.

Emily Nguyen was capturing every moment for her fans, as well as *Clearview's Morning Show* camera crew.

Instead of having the finalists make the same dish, Marieta had decided to choose a list of top-secret ingredients for them to make a Greek dish of their choosing. Then after the cookoff, the winner would be whomever she decided had the most inspiration from the gods.

But first she had to pick the finalists.

The atmosphere in *Aphrodite's* was electric with

anticipation as everyone gathered for Marieta's big announcement. The air was thick with the aroma of Greek spices and freshly baked bread, mingling with the excited chatter of the crowd.

I watched from my sanitized corner table as Marieta made her grand entrance, flanked by her imposing security detail. She looked every bit the celebrity chef in her crisp white chef's coat, her short dark hair perfectly styled. The crowd parted for her like the Red Sea, whispers and excited murmurs following in her wake.

Nik, Jaz, and Boomer sat with me, as I tried to keep my anxiety at bay in the crowded space. My thoughtful fiancé squeezed my hand reassuringly, sensing my discomfort, which only made me love him more.

Ma bustled around, her face flushed with excitement and nerves. She kept smoothing down her apron and adjusting the plates on the tables, muttering Greek prayers under her breath. Pop followed behind her, trying to calm her down, but she swatted his hands away every time he tried to touch her.

"Ophelia, relax," he said for the hundredth time. "Everything look good."

"It have to be more than good. It have to be perfect," Ma hissed back. "This Marieta Galanis. She big deal in Greek cooking world. We no embarrass ourselves in front of her." Ma adjusted her beehive and took a deep breath.

Marieta Galanis stood at the front of the restaurant, her presence commanding everyone's attention. Her sleek black hair was topped with a chef's hat, and she wore an immaculate, gleaming white chef's jacket adorned with the *Hades' Kitchen* logo.

"Ladies and gentlemen," she began, her voice carrying across the packed restaurant. "After careful consideration of all the entries, I am pleased to announce our two finalists for the *Hades' Kitchen* cookoff."

The crowd held its collective breath.

"Our first finalist is ..." Marieta paused for dramatic effect, "Ophelia Ballas!"

A cheer erupted from the Greek contingent. Ma beamed with pride, accepting hugs and congratulations from her family and friends.

"And our second finalist," Marieta continued once the noise died down, "is Vincenzo Ricci!"

The restaurant erupted in a mix of cheers and gasps at the announcement of the two finalists, as well as a few grumbled from those chefs not chosen. Ma's face registered shock before quickly morphing into steely determination. Vincenzo, for his part, looked equally surprised but pleased.

"Mama Mia!" Vincenzo exclaimed, his accent getting thicker with his excitement. He stood as tall as he could with his short, stocky frame. "I'll show you Greeks how it's a really done!"

Ma's eyes narrowed. "We see about that, you Italian imposter." Her face turned beet red as she glared daggers at Vincenzo, her hands flying about as she talked. "He no even Greek!" she protested loudly.

"Now, now," Marieta said, holding up her hands to quiet the crowd. "The beauty of cooking is that it transcends borders. This competition is about skill and creativity, not nationality. Let's keep things friendly. This is all in good fun, after all." She smiled, but there was a glint in her eye that suggested she was enjoying the drama.

Ma huffed but held her tongue, shooting one last glare at Vincenzo before plastering on a smile for the cameras.

"The cookoff will take place in one week," Marieta announced. "Our finalists will be given a list of secret ingredients and two hours to create their best Greek-inspired dish on that day. May the best chef win!"

"You heard it, folks," Emily said into her phone as she held it with a long-handled selfie stick and panned the room close to our table. "I can't wait to see what ingredients Chef Marieta comes up with."

Jasper walked by and waved to us. Not one to miss an opportunity, eagle-eyed Ma snagged him and pulled him in front of the camera.

"And this my son, Jasper," Ma announced proudly with a death grip on his arm so he couldn't get away. "He single and looking for nice Greek girl." She winked at Emily. "Or maybe nice travel blogger girl who want to settle down in quaint town."

Jasper's face flushed bright red. "Ma. Stop trying to set me up with every woman you meet." He gave Emily an apologetic look. "I'm so sorry about this."

Emily laughed good-naturedly. "No worries. Your mom seems great. But just so you know, we *are* live." She waved to her millions of followers and flushed over the comments speculating on a new romance rolling in across her screen before turning her camera to capture Ma's beaming face and changing the subject. "So, Mrs. Ballas, how do you feel about being chosen as a finalist?"

Ma's chest puffed up with pride. "I blessed by the gods themselves. My yiayia's recipes no fail me. That Vincenzo may know his way around pasta dish, but Greek cuisine? I no think so."

Vincenzo's face turned as red as his famous marinara sauce as he stormed over. "Pasta dish? I can cook circles around you, Ophelia Ballas. I'll have you know my moussaka would make your taste buds dance the tarantella!"

"Tarantella?" Ma scoffed, looking down her nose at him. "More like funeral dirge for you culinary aspirations."

"Ladies and gentlemen," Marieta interjected smoothly, clearly enjoying the spectacle, "let's save this spirited competition for the kitchen, shall we? Remember, cooking is about bringing people together, not dividing them."

With that, Emily signed off and Jasper retreated to the kitchen. As the excitement from the announcement died down, I noticed Bjorn slip away from the crowd and head towards the back of the restaurant.

What was he up to? I excused myself from our table and followed him discreetly. I found him in a quiet corner near the kitchen, speaking in hushed tones on his phone. Careful not to be seen, I edged closer to listen.

"... I know, I know," Bjorn was saying, his voice tense. "The police keep asking questions, and Nik ... he's not going to let this go."

There was a pause as he listened to the person on the other end.

"No, I haven't told him anything. But he's smart, he'll figure it out eventually." Another pause. "Look, we need to speed things up. Get everything in place as soon as possible and make our move."

"And what move is that, Mr. Stevens?" I asked from behind him.

He flinched, dropping his phone.

I picked it up and handed it to him, holding on for a moment, our hands touching.

"Just business, jente." *You probably won't believe me any more than my son. I would never harm a woman or knowingly swindle people, but you can be sure I will find out who did. Aye, it would be a darn sight easier if I could stop protecting people.* "Please, call me Bjorn."

I let go of the phone and crossed my arms, asking softly, "How are you holding up, Bjorn?"

He shrugged his massive shoulders. "I'm okay."

"Well, hang in there. For what it's worth, your son believes you didn't kill Sigrid, and so do I."

His eyes widened, and he took a step back as he looked at me warily. "How did you know I was thinking that?"

Whoops. I lifted a shoulder. "It's written all over your face," I hedged. "I suggest you never play poker."

He sighed. "I admit I'm not a very good liar." He held up his hands. "What you see is what you get."

"Then why not tell Nik what's really going on?"

"I can't. I might not be a liar, but I never break my word." He glanced at his phone as it buzzed. "If you'll excuse me, I have to go."

"Let us know if you need something," I hollered after him.

He paused and looked back at me. "Just my son. That's all I need." And then he was gone.

~

LATER THAT NIGHT, Nik and I were walking Willow and Wolfgang down Main Street. I was leash training Willow, while Nik was reigning Wolfgang in.

My mind raced with questions over my conversation with Nik's father. Bjorn's thoughts had confirmed he wasn't involved in Sigrid's murder, but he was clearly mixed up in something he felt he couldn't share. The protective instinct in his thoughts was strong—but who was he protecting?

And from what?

As I mulled over this new information, I felt Nik's eyes on me. I glanced over at him, his expression a mix of concern and curiosity.

"Everything okay, Ballas?" he asked, his eyes searching mine. "I saw you follow Pop back at *Aphrodite's.*"

I hesitated for a moment, wanting to be honest with Nik. "I ... I overheard part of a phone conversation he was having," I admitted finally. "Nik, I don't think your father killed Sigrid. He's definitely involved in something but not murder. I know your relationship is a little rocky, but he needs you. He seems a bit stressed. Maybe you should check on him."

Nik's brow furrowed. "Yeah, maybe I should." He sighed, running a hand through his hair. "This whole situation is just ... complicated."

I squeezed Nik's hand reassuringly. "I know it's complicated, but we'll figure it out together. That's what couples do. Your father may be hiding something, but I truly believe he's not a murderer."

Nik nodded, a small smile tugging at his lips. "Thanks, Ballas. I appreciate your support." He paused, his expression turning thoughtful. "You know, maybe I should try talking to him again. Really listen this time, without my detective hat on."

"I think that's a great idea, Detective," I said with a wink encouragingly. "Sometimes people just need to know they're being heard."

As we continued our walk, the dogs suddenly perked up, their noses twitching in the air. Wolfgang let out a low growl, pulling at his leash, Willow hot on his heels.

"Whoa, boy," Nik said, tightening his grip. "What's got you so excited?"

I scanned the area, my eyes narrowing as I spotted a figure lurking in the shadows near the church. "Nik, look," I whispered, nodding in that direction.

Nik followed my gaze, his body tensing. "Stay here with the dogs," he murmured, already moving towards the shadowy figure.

But before Nik could reach them, the person darted away, disappearing around the corner of the church. Nik broke into a run, pursuing the mystery figure.

My heart raced as I watched Nik disappear from view. The dogs whined, sensing the tension. I debated for a moment before making a decision.

"Come on, guys," I said to Wolfgang and Willow, tugging gently on their leashes. "Let's go make sure Daddy's okay."

We moved cautiously towards the church, the dogs alert and on guard. As we rounded the corner, I saw Nik standing alone, looking frustrated.

"They got away," he said as we approached. "Too quick and they knew the area well. There are all sorts of hiding places around here."

"Did you get a good look at them?" I asked, trying to keep my voice steady despite my racing heart.

Nik shook his head. "Not really. Medium height, slim build. Wearing all black with a hood up. Could have been anyone."

I puckered my brow, glancing around the dimly lit church grounds. "What do you think they were doing here?"

"No idea." Nik frowned, rubbing his whiskered jaw. "But given everything that's been happening, I don't like it. We should report this to Father Papadopoulos in the morning, see if anything's been disturbed."

As we turned to leave, Wolfgang suddenly stiffened, his nose twitching. Before either of us could react, he lunged forward with a powerful bark, dragging Nik along behind him.

"Wolfgang, heel!" Nik shouted, but the massive Saint Bernard was on a mission.

We chased after him, Willow yipping excitedly as she bounced along beside me. Wolfgang led us to a thick cluster of bushes near the church's side entrance. He began pawing at the ground, whining insistently.

"What is it, boy?" Nik asked, crouching down beside his dog, pulling out a small evidence bag from his pocket. "Perks of the job. I'm always packing something," he said with a wry smile as he carefully picked up the object.

It was a small, ornate key, intricately designed with what looked like serpents intertwined around the handle.

"That's ... unusual," I said, peering at the key. "Any idea what it might be for?"

Nik shook his head, bagging the key. "No, but I have a feeling it might be important. I'll have it analyzed at the lab tomorrow."

As we made our way home, my mind was racing. The mysterious figure, the strange key—it all seemed to point to something bigger going on.

The question was ... what?

9

It was the start of the Clearview County Fair. In Clearview, the fair wasn't just rides, games, and food trucks. All the businesses and restaurants in town had vender booths and food trucks on display.

The fair was packed.

Nik and Boomer were canvasing the fairgrounds, which were held in the park, looking for any leads on the case.

Jaz and I were setting up our staff at our *Full Disclosure* and *Kalli Originals* booth. Aunt Tasoula was making last minute touches to her hair products display and service packages in her *Hera's Halo* booth. Tate was counting his register in his *Hemsworth Hardware* booth.

Business Bend was a cul-de-sac at the end of Restaurant Row.

Meanwhile, on Restaurant Row, Silas and Kosmos had the sandwich station for their *Diner Delights* truck prepped and ready to go. I could smell Maria's famous cinnamon rolls and coffee in her *Sinfully Delicious* truck. And Michael had even tapped the kegs in *Flannigan's Pub* truck.

The only people falling behind the eight ball were

Aphrodite's and *Vincenzo's*. Their food trucks were right next to each other. No matter what one truck did, the other truck tried to outdo.

"Look at this spanakopita!" Ma proclaimed loudly, holding up a tray of golden, flaky pastries. "Made with spinach so fresh, you still hear it photosympathisizing!"

Not to be outdone, Vincenzo countered by dramatically unveiling a massive pot of sauce. "Behold, my world-famous marinara! So authentic, it makes Italians weepa with joy!"

Ma scoffed, her eyes narrowing. "Weep with joy? More like weep from heartburn. My tzatziki soothe they poor, abused stomachs."

"Tzatziki?" Vincenzo retorted. "That glorified yogurt dip? My pesto will a show them true flavora!"

As the two continued their culinary showdown, attracting a growing crowd of amused onlookers, I couldn't help but shake my head. The rivalry between Ma and Vincenzo had reached new heights since the announcement of the *Hades' Kitchen* finalists.

"I swear, those two are going to set the whole fair on fire with their competitiveness," Jaz said, chuckling as she arranged some clothing displays in our booth.

I nodded, carefully wiping down our counter for the third time. "At least it's good for business. Look at the crowd they're drawing."

Just then, Marieta Galanis herself strolled by, flanked by her ever-present security detail. She paused in front of Ma and Vincenzo's dueling food trucks, an amused smile playing on her lips.

"Well, well," she said, her voice carrying over the crowd. "It seems our finalists are giving us a little preview of the competition. How marvelous!"

Ma and Vincenzo immediately straightened up,

their faces flushing with a mix of pride and embarrassment.

"Ms. Galanis," Ma said, smoothing her apron. "We just getting warmed up for big competition."

"Indeed," Marieta replied, her eyes twinkling. "And what a warm-up it is. I look forward to seeing what you both bring to the actual cookoff."

"You want to try my spanakopita?" Ma held out the tray enticingly.

"Or perhaps you'd prefer a taste of true Italian cuisine?" Vincenzo interjected, brandishing a spoon full of his marinara sauce.

Marieta held up her hands, chuckling. "Now, now, save some of that competitive spirit for the actual competition. But I must say, I'm impressed by the passion I'm seeing here. It bodes well for an exciting cookoff."

"Have you chosen the secret ingredients yet?" a reporter asked.

"Now they wouldn't be secret if I told you, would they?" She winked. "You all will have to wait until the cookoff to find out."

As Marieta moved on, followed by a trail of eager fans and local reporters, I noticed Samuel Brooks lurking near the edge of the crowd, his keen eyes taking in every detail of the scene. When he caught me looking his way, he gave a slight nod before disappearing into the crowd.

"Did you see that?" I murmured to Jaz, pointing in the direction Samuel had vanished. The man was up to something.

"See what?" Jaz asked, looking up from arranging a display of scarves.

"Samuel Brooks. He was watching Ma and Vincenzo's little showdown pretty intently." I frowned, a nagging feeling settling in my gut. First, Bjorn and now my ma. "I wonder what angle he's working on this time."

Jaz shrugged. "Probably just looking for his next big scoop. You know how reporters are."

"Maybe," I said, unconvinced. "I don't trust the guy. Something about this whole situation feels off."

Before I could ponder it further, Nik appeared at our booth, looking slightly harried. "Hey, ladies. How's business?"

"Just getting started, but I have high hopes for a successful day," Jaz replied cheerfully. "How's the investigation going?"

Nik sighed, running a hand over his five o'clock shadow. "We're trying to keep an eye out for any suspicious activity, but with this many people around, it's like looking for a flea in Wolfgang's fur. Impossible."

I studied his face, noting the tension around his eyes. "Speaking of Wolfgang, any luck with that key he found?"

"Yes. The lab's still analyzing it," Nik replied, nodding. "But get this—apparently, it's made of an unusual alloy. Not something you'd find at your average hardware store. It looks ancient."

"Interesting," I mused. "Could it be connected to that old smuggling network Professor Grant mentioned?"

Nik shrugged. "It's possible. We're looking into it. Speaking of which, have either of you seen anything out of the ordinary today?"

Jaz and I exchanged glances. "Well, Samuel Brooks was lurking around," I said. "He seemed very interested in Ma and Vincenzo's rivalry."

Nik's brow furrowed. "Brooks again?" He shook his head. "That guy's been popping up everywhere lately."

"You don't think he could be involved somehow and maybe just trying to shift attention and cover his tracks, do you?" Jaz asked, lowering her voice.

"I'm not ruling anything out at this point," Nik replied grimly. "But let's not jump to conclusions. He is a journalist after all—could just be sniffing around for a story. The man is relentless, I'll give him that."

Just then, a commotion erupted from the direction of Ma and Vincenzo's food trucks. We all turned to see a crowd gathering, voices raised in alarm.

"We better check that out," Nik said, already moving towards the disturbance.

Jaz and I exchanged glances before following close behind. As we approached Ma and Vincenzo's food trucks, the crowd parted to reveal a shocking sight. Sprawled on the ground between the two trucks was a man, unconscious and pale.

Samuel Brooks.

"Oh, my Zeus," I gasped, my hand flying to my mouth.

Nik was already in action, crouching beside Samuel and checking for a pulse. "He's alive, but barely," he announced, his voice tense. "Someone call an ambulance!"

Ma hovered nearby, wringing her hands. "Me and Vinny ... we just argue like normal, then this guy come up. Ask questions. Then poof. He collapse!"

Vincenzo nodded vigorously in agreement for once. "Si, si! One minute he was fine, the next—bam! Down he went like a bad soufflé."

Nik's eyes narrowed as he scanned the area, taking note of the growing crowd. "Did anyone see what happened?"

A nervous murmur rippled through the onlookers, but no one stepped forward. I noticed Evangeline

Marinakis hovering at the edge of the group, her face pale and drawn. When she caught me looking, she quickly turned away.

"Alright, everyone please stay calm and give us some space," Nik announced, his authoritative voice cutting through the chatter. "Boomer, secure the area. This is now an active crime scene."

As Boomer began cordoning off the area with police tape, I knelt beside Nik, careful not to touch anything. "What do you think happened?" I whispered.

Nik shook his head slightly, his brow furrowed in concentration. "Not sure yet. No visible signs of trauma, but ..." He leaned in closer, his eyes narrowing as he examined Samuel's face. "Wait a second ..." He leaned over and peeked to the side of Samuel's head, revealing a small, red puncture mark just behind his ear.

My breath caught in my throat. "Is that ..."

"A snake bite," Nik confirmed grimly. "Looks like our venomous friend has struck again."

"A snake bite behind his ear? What did someone do ... throw it at him?" I looked at Nik, and his eyes were filled with the same concern in mine.

Just then, the wail of sirens cut through the air as an ambulance approached. Paramedics rushed in, quickly assessing Samuel's condition before loading him onto a stretcher and whisking him away to the hospital.

Nik and Boomer took everyone's statement while the CSI guys assessed the area, collecting evidence. Vinny was furious his food truck was shut down for the time being, insisting on talking with the mayor. Meanwhile, the mamas had disappeared.

That was never a good sign.

~

AFTER SALVAGING what remained of the day, Jaz and I left our booth in good hands with our assistants, while we wandered around the fair.

We passed the game area, full of bells and whistles and shouts of laughter and excitement as people won prizes. Further down, we traveled through the midway. All the rides were running, with children laughing and screaming as nervous parents looked on.

I was a little leery, knowing a poisonous snake was still on the loose. Clearview County Fair was one of our biggest moneymakers, and who knew how long it would take to catch this snake.

Mayor Zimmerman made a judgment call to the leave the fair open with a warning, giving people the option to leave or stay at their own risk. Several locals left, but many others chose to stay since most were snake enthusiasts who'd come to see the snakes anyway.

To them, a poisonous snake was the icing on the cake.

Natalie was called in with her team to search the area, but the park was big. We finally made it to the pond with the paddle boat rides. On the bridge over the pond, I saw Bjorn talking on the phone.

Who was he talking to this time?

Jaz and I slowed our pace, trying to casually observe Bjorn without drawing attention to ourselves. His body language was tense but not hostile—like whoever he was talking to, he was having an intense discussion with rather than an argument.

"What do you think that's about?" Jaz whispered, nodding subtly towards the pair on the bridge.

I shook my head slightly. "I'm not sure. He's been acting secretive and strange, according to Nik."

We pretended to be interested in the paddle boats, moving closer to try and overhear their conversation. The voices were too muffled.

"We need to get even closer," I whispered to Jaz, pulling her along with me. "Maybe we can overhear something."

Jaz nodded in agreement, hurrying to keep up. "Good idea, but slow down. Let's pretend we're just taking a stroll around the pond."

We slowed our walk, casually talking and pointing at things as we made our way towards the bridge, trying to appear nonchalant. As Jaz and I strolled closer to the bridge, snippets of Bjorn's conversation drifted our way.

"... can't let them get away with this," he was saying, his voice low but urgent. Now's the time to act before—"

He listened to whoever had interrupted him. "I know, I know," he interjected, throwing his huge hands up. "Samuel almost ruined our efforts."

He listened again, nodding. "I know Nik's getting too close, but trust me, he won't figure it out." Bjorn reassured the other person but didn't sound entirely convinced himself. "Nik's a good detective, but he doesn't have all the pieces."

Jaz and I exchanged a meaningful glance. What pieces was Bjorn referring to? And what exactly were they trying to keep hidden?

I blinked, looking around. "What's that sound?"

"I don't see anything, but it's coming from over there." Jaz pointed away from the bridge to a spot on the other side of the pond.

I glanced back at the bridge, but Bjorn was already

gone, headed that way as well. We hurried around the pond, following the sound.

"It's almost hypnotic," I said. "It sounds familiar, but I can't place where I've heard that."

"Yeah, like in a movie or something," Jaz added, then stopped short. "What in the world is that?"

A woman wearing a head scarf at least a foot high was swaying back and forth while playing a tiny flute like instrument. Only one thing could be under that scarf to make it sit so high.

Ma's beehive.

Jaz gaped. "Is that your Aunt Tasoula swinging her hips like that?"

"It sure looks it," I ground out.

"Listen to that rattling. Are those snake rattles hanging off her belt?"

"Where in Mount Olympus did she get those?" I sighed. "Come on." I kept walking closer, looking around for the third mama in the trio. Where one was, the other two weren't far behind.

Sure enough, there was Chloe walking along the bushes in a khaki button-down shirt and short set, socks scrunched down above hiking boots, and a wide brimmed hat. She wore gloves and held a large net in front of her, looking more ready to catch butterflies than a snake.

Suddenly, the music stopped.

Natalie and her team suddenly appeared from around the corner, and she didn't look happy. "Don't even tell me this is what I think it is."

"No, no. I won't. Okay? Okay." Aunt Tasoula kept swinging those hips. *Rattle. Rattle. Rattle.*

"'Soula, you nitwit. You gonna hurt youself." Ma sighed.

"What? You no think I charming, 'Phelia?" Aunt Tasoula put her hands on her hips.

"This snake no man, 'Soula. You gotta charm it with the pungi."

"I no use plungi. That for toilets." My aunt wrinkled her nose.

Ma rolled her eyes. "Pungi is instrument. It make music."

"Plungi make music too. Nasty music." Aunt Tasoula shuddered. "I use hips. I no meet male species who no like sweet hip music."

"Snakes no have hips, you nincompoop," Ma snapped.

This was my life, I thought, shaking my head.

"Well, someone charm them, so I can grab them with my net." Chloe kept scouring the bushes, her net ready in her hands before her.

"Chloe Stevens, what in the name of the gods are you doing? You're going to get yourself killed," Bjorn said as he joined them.

"Pagonis," she spat, "soon to be Crenshaw. I no Stevens ever again." She glared at him, looking around. "What, no woman?"

"There is no other woman," Bjorn said.

"What about you business partner," Chloe hissed.

"Partner schmartner," Ma chimed in. "A woman is a woman."

"That right," Aunt Tasoula said, swinging her hips in time to, "R.E.S.P.E.C.T."

Bjorn threw his hands up in defeat.

"Listen, ladies," Natalie butted in. "This has to stop. You can't try to catch a poisonous snake with hypnotic 'charming' and nets. That's a myth anyway. Please leave the snake catching to the professionals like me."

"And me," Bjorn added, stepping closer to Natalie. "I'm her assistant from time to time."

Chloe rolled her eyes.

Aunt Tasoula shook her head.

Ma grunted.

Something darted out of the bushes, making a hissing sound, and everyone ran screaming at once.

10

Jaz and I headed to *Clearview Hospital* that evening to check on Samuel.

On our way there, we passed *Rockwell Jewelers*. Milly Donovan-Rockwell ran *Dino's Doggy Daycare,* and managed the trainers at the park, and her work who trained all our pups, while Nelson ran the jewelry store. She and Nelson were married with a beautiful baby girl.

Jaz did a double take. "Was that Niles who just walked into *Rockwell Jewelers*?"

I glanced over my shoulder quickly. "That sure looks like him." Then I faced the road and kept driving.

"His wife is dead." Jaz frowned. "I wouldn't imagine even someone like him would move on that quickly to buy jewelry for another woman."

I shrugged. "Could be he's buying some for himself."

"Hmmm." Jaz shook her head. "He doesn't really seem the jewelry type."

"He did have an expensive watch. A lot of businessmen do." I suddenly remembered the snake key from the church. "What if he was the person dressed in black at the church the other night? He might have found another piece with that intricate serpent detailing. Nelson doesn't just sell fine jewelry. He sells unique, rare pieces as well."

"Hmm. I wonder if Milly knows anything about it? I'll have to text her later. She's training Armani tomorrow. That boy has way too much energy."

"I hear that. Willow doesn't stop moving all day and then crashes at night because she's so tired. Meanwhile, we're all exhausted right along with her."

"Amen to that." Jaz pointed out a parking spot at the hospital, and after parking, then locking the car, we headed inside.

Just outside Samuel's room, we came to a stop. Father Papadopoulos and Sister Philothea were inside. We exchanged surprised glances as we watched them speaking quietly with Samuel, who was propped up in the hospital bed looking pale but alert.

"What do you think that's about?" Jaz whispered.

I shook my head slightly. "Not sure, but it seems odd that Father would be visiting Samuel. As far as I know, Samuel isn't part of the church congregation."

We waited discreetly outside the room until Father and Sister finished their visit. As they exited, he looked surprised to see us, but nodded politely.

"Good evening, ladies," he said, his voice low. "I'm glad to see Samuel has visitors. He could use some friendly faces right now."

"Of course, Father," I replied and nodded a hello to the sister. "We just wanted to check on him. How is he doing?"

Father Papadopoulos sighed, his weathered face creasing with concern. "He's stable, thank goodness. The doctors were able to administer the antivenom in time. But it was a close call."

I nodded, glancing towards Samuel's room. "We're glad he's okay. If you don't mind me asking, Father, how do you know Samuel? I'm surprised to see you both here. I didn't realize he was part of the church community."

A flicker of something—discomfort? guilt?—passed over Father's face before he smoothed his expression. "Oh, well, Samuel has been doing some research on the church's history for an article. We've spoken a few times about the legend of the snakes in Greece and how some think that's what's happening in Clearview, among other things. Sister has been a big help. She might be new to the parish, but she's great with research."

Sister's face flushed pink, clearly uncomfortable with praise.

"I see," I said, not entirely convinced by his explanation. There seemed to be more to the story, but I didn't want to push.

"I'll wait for you outside," Sister said to Father and nodded farewell to us.

Father Papadopoulos smiled gently. "She's quite modest and a bit shy, but she's coming along. Well, I'll leave you ladies to your visit. Please, give Samuel my best."

As Father walked away, Jaz and I exchanged another meaningful glance before entering Samuel's hospital room.

Samuel looked up as we entered, his face brightening slightly despite his pale complexion. "Ms. Ballas, Ms. Alvarez. To what do I owe the pleasure?"

"We just wanted to check on you," I said, moving closer to his bedside. "How are you feeling?"

Samuel chuckled weakly. "Like I've been bitten by a venomous snake. But I suppose I should count myself lucky—I'm still here to talk about it."

Jaz nodded sympathetically. "How terrifying that must have been. Do you remember anything about what happened?"

Samuel's brow furrowed in concentration. "It's all a bit fuzzy, to be honest. I remember talking to Mrs. Ballas and Mr. Ricci about their cooking rivalry, then I walked away when they had customers. I was by a group of bushes when I felt a sharp pain behind my ear, and everything went black."

I exchanged a glance with Jaz before asking carefully, "Did you see anyone suspicious around before it happened? Or notice anything out of the ordinary?"

Samuel shook his head slowly. "Not that I can recall. But ..." he trailed off, his eyes growing distant.

"But what?" Jaz prompted gently.

Samuel hesitated, then sighed. "Look, I know I don't have the best reputation since I arrived in town. People think I'm just after a sensational story." He locked eyes with me. "But the truth is, I've been investigating something much bigger than some snake legend and cooking rivalry."

My mind raced with possibilities. "What do you mean, something bigger?"

Samuel glanced towards the door, as if checking to make sure we were alone. "I can't go into all the details right now, but let's just say there are some powerful people in this town with secrets they'd rather keep buried. And I think those secrets might be connected to what's been happening lately."

"The snake attacks?" Jaz asked, stepping closer to his bed.

Samuel nodded grimly. "Among other things. I've been piecing together evidence of an underground network operating in Clearview for years. A black market. And I think someone is willing to go to great lengths to keep it all under wraps."

I felt the hairs on the back of my neck stand at attention. "Do you think that's why you were attacked?"

"It's possible," Samuel replied. "I may have gotten too close to the truth. Or maybe someone wanted to send a message."

I exchanged a worried glance with Jaz. "Samuel, you should tell the police about this. If someone is targeting you—"

He held up a hand to stop me. "I appreciate your concern, but I can't go to the police yet. Not without concrete evidence. And frankly, I'm not sure who I can trust."

"What about Father Papadopoulos and Sister Philothea?" Jaz asked. "We saw them leaving as we arrived. Are they involved in your research somehow?"

A flicker of unease crossed Samuel's face. "Sister Philothea is very skilled at research. She's been a big help. Father Papadopoulos is ... complicated. Let's just say he knows more than he lets on about the history of this town and the church."

I lowered my voice. "Samuel, if you—"

"Excuse me, ladies, I'm going to have to ask you to leave," a nurse said as she entered the room. "I need to take Samuel's vitals, and he needs to rest."

"Certainly," I said, then looked over my shoulder before leaving the room. "Take care, Samuel. You know where we are if you want to talk."

He nodded once, then turned to look out the window.

And that was our cue to leave.

∾

LATER THAT EVENING, Nik and I brought our dogs over to Jaz and Boomer's house to play while we had drinks and caught up.

Jaz and Boomer had a really cute ranch on the outskirts of town. Initially, Jaz and I were roommates, but as our lives had grown to include our fiancés and even more fur babies, things had had to change. I missed the old days, but I was excited for our futures ... even if I wasn't so sure of my own. Pushing that thought out of my mind, I focused on their new house.

I really liked it.

The house was a beautiful ranch style with a neatly trimmed lawn and flower beds lining the walkway. The beige exterior was accented with white shutters and a rustic wooden door.

As we walked up the path to the house, I could smell a faint hint of freshly cut grass and flowers. The house was surrounded by a beautiful garden, full of colorful blooms and fragrant herbs.

Nik knocked and Boomer hollered for us to come on around back. Taking the dogs through the fence, we turned them loose and joined Jaz and Boomer on their patio. Jaz had set out a charcuterie board and handed me a glass of Chardonnay, while Boomer popped the top of a beer for Nik.

"So, how's the investigation going?" I asked, settling into a comfortable patio chair that Jaz had already sanitized for me.

Nik sighed, taking a long swig of his beer. "We're still waiting on the lab results from that key Wolfgang found. And now with Samuel's attack, we've got even more questions than answers."

Boomer nodded grimly. "It's like every time we think we're getting close to something, another wrench gets thrown in the works."

"Speaking of Samuel," Jaz said, exchanging a glance with me, "Kalli and I visited him in the hospital today."

Nik's eyebrows shot up. "You did? What did he have to say?"

I recounted our conversation with Samuel, watching as Nik and Boomer's expressions grew increasingly concerned.

"An underground network?" Boomer repeated, his brow furrowed.

Nik put his hand on my knee. *This is why I don't want you involved, Ballas.*

I squeezed Nik's hand reassuringly, silently letting him know I understood his concern. But I couldn't just sit idly by when there was so much at stake.

"I know it sounds far-fetched," I said, "but given everything that's been happening, it's not outside the realm of possibility."

Nik nodded slowly. "You're right. And it does line up with some of the rumors we've been hearing. The question is, how deep does this go? And who's involved?"

"That's what we need to figure out," Boomer added, leaning forward intently. "If there really is some kind of black-market operation in Clearview, it could explain a lot—the rare snake, the attacks, maybe even Sigrid's murder."

Jaz frowned. "But how does the church fit into all this? Samuel seemed to think Father Papadopoulos knows more than he's letting on."

Nik ran a hand through his hair, his expression troubled. "That's another piece of the puzzle we need to figure out. The church has been at the center of a lot of this—the snakes, the land disputes, and now possibly some connection to an underground network. We need to tread carefully there, especially with our families."

"It would send the mamas off the deep end," Boomer grunted.

"What about your father, Nik?" I asked gently. "Jaz and I saw him talking on the phone at the fair today. His conversation seemed ... intense."

Nik's jaw clenched slightly. "Pop's still not being forthcoming. I tried talking to him like you suggested, Kalli, but he just keeps insisting he can't tell me everything for my own protection."

"Protection from what though?" Jaz asked, voicing the question we were all thinking.

Nik shook his head in frustration. "That's the million-dollar question. He won't give me a straight answer."

I chewed my lip thoughtfully. "Do you think it could be connected to this underground network Samuel mentioned? I hate to say it, but maybe your father got mixed up in something he shouldn't have."

"It's possible," Nik admitted reluctantly. "Maybe that's why his ex-business partner, Ingrid, was so mad. But I can't imagine Pop being involved in anything truly illegal. He may be a lot of things, but he's not a criminal. I wish he had an alibi. Driving around alone all night and not getting back to the hotel until morning doesn't look good."

"Maybe he's trying to protect someone else," Boomer suggested. "Or maybe he's in over his head and doesn't know how to get out."

We all fell silent for a moment, contemplating the possibilities. The only sounds were the distant barking of the dogs playing in the yard and the gentle clinking of ice in our glasses.

"Well," I said finally, "it seems like we have a lot

more questions than answers at this point. But at least we're starting to see some connections, even if we don't fully understand them yet."

Nik nodded, squeezing my hand. "You're right. And as much as I hate to admit it, your sleuthing has uncovered some valuable information. You two have connections in this town. People trust you. They talk to you." He gave me a wry smile. "Just promise me you'll be careful, okay? Whoever's behind all this clearly isn't afraid to resort to violence."

"I promise," I said solemnly. "No unnecessary risks."

"That goes for you too," Boomer said to Jaz, who rolled her eyes good-naturedly.

"Yes, dear," she replied, then added, "Now, let's make a plan."

"Why do I feel like we're going to regret this?" Boomer said to Nik.

"History, brother. History." They clinked bottles, while Jaz and I headed inside for a refill and to talk behind their backs, of course.

Before we could say a word, Jaz's phone rang.

"Hi, Milly, so you got my text earlier?" Jaz put her phone on speaker.

"Yes. You'll never believe what just happened," she exclaimed.

"I have you on speaker. Kalli's here. What's wrong?" Jaz asked, concern evident in her voice. "Is everything okay?"

"Oh yes, everything's fine. It's just ... well, you mentioned that strange man who came into Nelson's jewelry store that you and Kalli saw earlier."

I exchanged a glance with Jaz. "Kalli here, Milly. You mean Niles Turner?"

"Hi, Kalli. Yes, that's the one," Milly confirmed.

"Well, Nelson said he was in yesterday and then he came back today when you saw him, right as Nelson was closing up shop. And you won't believe what he was looking for," Milly continued, her voice brimming with excitement she couldn't hide.

Jaz and I leaned in closer to the phone. "What was it?" I asked.

"A very specific type of antique key," Milly replied. "Nelson said it was unlike anything he'd ever seen before. Apparently, it had some kind of intricate snake design on it."

Jaz and I exchanged shocked glances. "A snake key?" Jaz repeated. "Like the one Wolfgang found near the church?"

"Exactly," Milly confirmed. "Nelson said Niles seemed really interested in finding it. He was offering an obscene amount of money for any information about where he could get one."

My mind was racing. "Did Nelson have anything like that?"

"No," Milly said. "He told Niles he'd never seen anything like it before. But get this—Niles left his contact information in case Nelson came across one or heard about one. And he seemed pretty confident there might be more than one."

More than one? I had a sudden premonition the key at the lab would unlock a lot of the answers we were looking for. "Milly, this is really important information. Would you mind if we shared it with Nik and Boomer?"

"Of course not," Milly replied. "I figured it might be relevant to the investigation. That's why I called as soon as Nelson told me about it."

"Thank you so much, Milly," Jaz said. "You may have just given us a huge lead."

11

The next day I walked into my aunt's hair salon, *Hera's Halo*, to drop off some snacks for her customers. Ma was cooking up a storm, making all sorts of Greek dishes in preparation for the cookoff.

Marieta still hadn't given the contestants the secret ingredients. That didn't stop Ma. She had put her Greek phone tree to work. She had spies all over town keeping their eyes peeled on where Marieta was shopping.

Marieta hadn't hit *Stallone's Supermarket*, choosing instead to frequent unique mom and pop food stands, an unconventional butcher with a wide array of meat, whole food and organic shops, and the farmer's market. So, Ma was guessing at all the possible combinations, trying traditional recipes with new twists of her own.

The salon was busy like it always was. Aunt Tasoula had cut and colored Evangeline's hair and had just put her under the dryer.

She took the box from me and inhaled deeply. "This smell so good. I love it when Ophelia get stressed."

"You do?" I asked, my eyebrows arching high.

She nodded once and shot me a wink. "It mean I eat good." She carried the box around the salon, handing out food.

I followed her, chuckling.

People raved over what they were tasting.

I smiled as I watched the customers enjoying Ma's cooking. Aunt Tasoula was right—Ma's stress baking and cooking did have its perks.

As Aunt Tasoula made her rounds with the snacks, I looked back at Evangeline sitting under the dryer, flipping through a magazine. She seemed tense, her shoulders hunched, and her brow furrowed. I decided to seize the opportunity to chat with her.

"Hi Evangeline," I said, approaching her chair. "How are you doing?"

She looked up, startled. "Oh, Kalli. I'm fine, thank you." She hesitated, then added, "I'm just a bit worried about everything that's been happening in town lately."

I nodded sympathetically. "It has been quite unsettling. The snake attacks, Samuel Brooks in the hospital ... it's a lot to take in."

Her face paled at the mention of Samuel. "The streets aren't safe in Clearview anymore, and no one is doing anything."

"Detective Stevens and Detective Matheson are working hard on finding Sigrid's killer and catching the poisonous snake."

"Well, hopefully there's only one. It could be anywhere." She shuddered.

"You were right by Samuel when he got bit. Did you see anything?"

Evangeline's eyes widened slightly at my question. She glanced around nervously before lowering her voice. "I ... I'm not sure," she said in a whisper voice. "Everything happened so fast. One moment Samuel was talking to Mrs. Ballas and Mr. Ricci, then standing by the bushes, and then suddenly he just collapsed." She wrung her hands anxiously. "It was terrifying."

I nodded encouragingly. "I can imagine. Did you notice anyone suspicious hanging around before it happened?"

Evangeline hesitated, her brow furrowing in concentration. "Well, now that you mention it ... I did see someone lurking near the food trucks just before Samuel approached. They were wearing dark clothes and a hat pulled low over their face. I thought it was odd, given how hot it was that day."

My pulse quickened at this new information. "Do you remember anything else about this person? Height, build, anything distinctive?"

Evangeline closed her eyes, as if trying to recall the details. "They were average height, I'd say. Not too tall or short. Average build. I couldn't see their face clearly, but ..." She trailed off, looking uncertain.

"But what?" I prompted gently.

She lowered her voice to barely above a whisper. "I could have sworn I saw something glinting in their hand. Like metal catching the sunlight. At first, I thought it might have been a phone, but now I'm not so sure."

My mind raced with possibilities. Could it have been the snake key? Or perhaps some kind of tool used to handle the venomous snake? "Thank you, Evangeline," I said sincerely. "This could be really helpful information. I'll pass it on to the police."

"I hope you do that." She pursed her lips. "Lord knows Father and his staff aren't doing enough to stop the madness. The church is becoming a mockery. I can only imagine what might happen next."

"What next? You see new special hairdo," Aunt Tasoula said.

"I have to say whatever brand of color you used this time must be strong. My scalp is tingling all over," Evangeline said.

"No new brand. Same as always." Aunt Tasoula shrugged as she lifted the dryer. "I make you look like … Medusa?" Her eyes sprang wide, and she covered them with her hand as she turned Evangeline toward the mirror. "I sorry. Please no turn me to stone."

Evangeline screamed.

I gasped.

Tiny little snakes were woven throughout her hair, wiggling away, making her look like she was standing in a windstorm. Aunt Tasoula peeked through her fingers and then made the sign of the cross.

I looked around the salon as customers started to scream.

Snakes were emerging from everywhere. I stood frozen in shock as chaos erupted around me. Tiny snakes were slithering out from under chairs, emerging from potted plants, and even dropping from light fixtures. Women were screaming and jumping onto chairs, their hair half-done and foils flying.

"Oh, my Zeus!" Aunt Tasoula shrieked, wielding a hairbrush like a weapon. "Where they come from?"

Evangeline was hyperventilating, her eyes wide with terror as she stared at her reflection. The snakes in her hair seemed to be multiplying by the second.

I snapped out of my stupor and sprang into action.

"Everyone stay calm!" I shouted, though my own heart was racing. "These look like harmless garden snakes. Let's get everyone out of here safely."

As I helped usher panicked customers towards the exit, I pulled out my phone to call Nik. My fingers trembled as I dialed his number.

"Ballas? What's wrong?" Nik's voice came through, instantly alert.

"Nik, you need to get to *Hera's Halo* right away," I said, trying to keep my voice steady. "There are snakes everywhere. Dozens of them."

"What? Are you okay?" I could hear the concern and urgency in his voice.

"I'm fine, but it's pandemonium here. These look like garden snakes, not venomous, but we need help getting everyone out safely and figuring out where they came from."

"I'm on my way," Nik said. "Stay safe and try to keep everyone calm. I'll be there in five minutes."

As I hung up, I turned to see Aunt Tasoula corralling snakes with a broom, muttering Greek curses under her breath. Evangeline was still frozen in her chair, whimpering as she stared at her reflection.

"Aunt Tasoula, leave the snakes for now," I called out. "We need to focus on getting everyone out safely."

She nodded, abandoning her snake-herding efforts to help an elderly customer down from where she had climbed onto a styling chair.

I made my way over to Evangeline, careful to avoid stepping on any slithering creatures. "Evangeline, we need to get you out of here. Can you stand?"

She shook her head vigorously, causing the snakes in her hair to wiggle more. "I can't move! They're all over me!"

"It's okay," I said soothingly, though my own skin was crawling. I wanted to help her, but I couldn't bring myself to touch the snakes. "They're just garden snakes," I reminded her for both our sakes. "They won't hurt you." That didn't stop me from trembling with the thought of what germs I might encounter. I took a deep breath, stealing myself. "Okay, Evangeline. I'm going to help you up slowly. Just focus on me, not the snakes."

Carefully, I reached out and grasped her arms, avoiding touching her snake-infested hair. With gentle coaxing, I managed to get her to her feet. She clung to me, shaking like a leaf, and I tried not to think about being this close to her.

"That's it," I encouraged with my most soothing tone, as much for me as for her. "Tilt your head forward and shake hard."

She tried to no avail.

I looked around for something to maneuver them out of her hair, but nothing seemed long enough, and the snakes were tangled up good. This was beyond my capabilities. There was nothing left to do except get her outside.

"We're going to walk to the door, nice and slow, okay?"

She nodded.

I held her arm as we inched our way across the salon floor, dodging snakes at every step. Evangeline whimpered with each movement, but we kept going. *I should have finished what I started. Then none of this would be happening. I will finish, just as soon as...*

Nik burst in through the door, followed by Boomer and animal control, startling us both. We jerked apart, and I lost her thought.

"Kalli!" Nik exclaimed, rushing over to us. His eyes widened as he took in Evangeline's Medusa hairdo.

Boomer let out a little yelp and headed in the opposite direction, leaving Natalie and her crew to take care of the hissing mess.

Nik quickly took charge of the situation, coordinating with animal control to safely remove the snakes while Boomer helped escort the remaining customers out. I stayed with Evangeline, trying to keep her calm as animal control carefully extracted the snakes from her now tangled hair.

"Where could all these snakes have come from?" I wondered aloud as things began to settle down.

Nik frowned, surveying the scene. "That's what we need to figure out. This many snakes don't just appear out of nowhere. Someone must have planted them here."

"But who would do such a thing? And why?" I asked, my mind racing with possibilities.

"I don't know," Nik replied grimly. "But I have a feeling it's connected to everything else that's been happening. We need to figure this out before anything else—"

Nik's phone buzzed. He frowned as he answered, "Detective Stevens here." His eyes widened as he listened. "When did this happen?" He rubbed his jaw and shook his head. "Okay, I'm on it." Then he hung up.

"What's wrong?"

"That was Captain Crenshaw. Your aunt's place wasn't the only place targeted."

I blinked. "What do you mean?"

"Several businesses are overrun with snakes right now, and they all have one thing in common."

"What's that?"

"They're all Greek. It seems our perpetrator is trying to send a message."

"The question is, what?"

A movement by the street caught my eye. I turned to look and saw Evangeline peeling away from the curb in a hurry. I couldn't help but wonder if she was off to finish what she started ... whatever that was.

I LEFT *Hera's Halo* with the intent to go into work, but a hunch had me heading to *Holy Trinity Greek Orthodox Church*. Nik and Boomer were back at my aunt's salon, looking for clues, and Jaz was at the boutique.

This was my chance to do a little solo investigating.

I pulled my Prius into the parking lot, and sure enough, there was Evangeline's car. Scanning the yard, I saw Yanni's crew working on the landscaping with Dale while Tate's crew was fixing up the cracks in the building with Cole.

I slipped inside. It was tranquil and quiet being in church outside of mass. I walked down the aisle toward the altar and heard voices in the back near the confessionals.

I edged forward and peeked around the corner. Evangeline was with Father Papadopoulos. She was asking him to bless her after her traumatic Medusa hairdo experience.

I crept closer, straining to hear their conversation.

"... can't go on like this," Evangeline was saying, her voice trembling. "The snakes, the attacks—it's all getting out of hand. We need to do something before someone else gets hurt."

Father Papadopoulos sighed heavily. "I understand your concern, Evangeline. But we must have faith that the authorities will resolve this situation. In the meantime, we must pray for guidance and protection."

"Prayers aren't enough anymore, Father," Evangeline snapped. "You know as well as I do that there's more going on here than just some ancient legend in Greece coming to life in Clearview. The truth needs to come out before it's too late."

I strained to hear better, my heart racing. What truth was Evangeline referring to?

"Evangeline, please," Father Papadopoulos said, "you're letting your imagination run away with you. I suggest you take some time off. Maybe stay away from the church for a bit for your own good."

Evangeline's voice rose, tinged with desperation. "My own good? What about the good of the church? Of the whole town? Father, we can't keep pretending—"

She cut off abruptly as I accidentally bumped into a nearby pew, causing a small scraping sound. I froze, holding my breath.

"Who's there?" Father Papadopoulos called out.

Knowing I was caught, I stepped out from my hiding spot. "I'm so sorry to interrupt," I said, trying to look casual. "I just came in to ... pray."

Father Papadopoulos and Evangeline exchanged a tense glance before Father plastered on a smile. "Of course, Kalli. The church is always open for those seeking solace. Evangeline and I were just finishing up."

Evangeline nodded stiffly, her eyes darting between Father Papadopoulos and me. "Yes, I should be going. Thank you for your time, Father." She turned to leave, then paused, looking back at me. "Thank you for your help at the salon, Kalli. And please ... be careful."

With that cryptic warning, she hurried out of the church, leaving me alone with Father Papadopoulos. An uncomfortable silence settled between us.

"Is everything alright, Father?" I asked, trying to sound casual. "Evangeline seemed quite upset."

Father Papadopoulos sighed, rubbing his temples. "Evangeline is ... passionate about the church and its traditions. Sometimes that passion can lead her to see conspiracies where there are none. The recent events have everyone on edge."

I nodded, not entirely convinced.

"I can understand that," I said carefully. "These snake incidents have everyone rattled. Speaking of which, I noticed Yanni and his crew working on the grounds. Are they doing anything special to try to prevent more snakes from getting onto the property?"

Father Papadopoulos gave me a tired smile. "They're doing what they can—sealing up any cracks or holes, clearing dense vegetation where snakes might hide. But of course, we can't completely snake-proof the entire grounds."

I nodded thoughtfully. "And what about inside the church? Have there been any ... unusual discoveries in here?"

The priest's eyes narrowed slightly. "What exactly are you asking, Kalli?"

I shrugged, trying to appear nonchalant. "Oh, you know, just curious if anything strange has happened. Secret passages, hidden rooms, that sort of thing."

"You've seen too many movies, my dear." His eyes darted away at a noise he heard down the hall. I could have sworn I saw black robes flash by. "If you'll excuse me, I have some duties to attend to." He nodded once. "I expect to see you and your family at the service this week despite the incidents. We all need to band together if we're going to save our parish."

"Of course, father," I called after him as he hurried

down the hall in the same direction as the noise we'd heard.

What was his hurry, and what duties did he have to attend to?

12

Today was the day.

The cookoff was about to begin. The scene at *Aphrodite's* was a feast for the eyes. The restaurant was bustling with activity, as Marieta's assistants in various uniforms hurried in and out of the kitchen.

Security manned the corners of the room, and *The Clearview Morning Show* cameras were panned and ready for the event to begin.

The vibrant reds, greens, and yellows of the Greek flags and decorations adorned the walls and tables at *Aphrodite's*.

Ma stood tall and proud in her crisp white chef's uniform, embroidered with the Greek flag and adorned with golden olive leaves. Vinny's uniform was just as crisp, but in a bold red and white checkered pattern, representing his Italian heritage.

The two chefs stood behind their own portable cooking stations that had been set up at the front of the dining room, compliments of the morning show. They had been provided with state-of-the-art supplies encompassing everything they would need for the battle in the kitchen.

The host of the morning show, Rebecca Robinson, stood next to Marieta with microphone in hand as the news producer counted her down until they were on the air.

Rebecca smiled brightly at the camera as the producer signaled they were live. "Good morning, Clearview! We're coming to you from *Aphrodite's* restaurant for the highly anticipated *Hades' Kitchen* cookoff! I'm Rebecca Robinson, and with me is the one and only Marieta Galanis, celebrity chef extraordinaire and judge for today's competition."

Marieta nodded graciously. "Thank you, Rebecca. I'm thrilled to be here in Clearview for this exciting event."

"The tension is palpable here in *Aphrodite's*," Rebecca continued. "Our two finalists, Ophelia Ballas and Vincenzo Ricci, are ready to battle it out in the kitchen. Marieta, can you tell us what challenge awaits our chefs today?"

Marieta's eyes twinkled mischievously. "Well, Rebecca, I've prepared a special challenge for our finalists today. They'll be working with a unique combination of ingredients that celebrate both Greek and Italian cuisines, with a twist that pays homage to the ancient Greek snake legend."

Rebecca's eyebrows shot up. "Intriguing! Can you give us a hint about these secret ingredients?"

Marieta shook her head, smiling. "You'll have to wait and see, just like our contestants. But I can say that they'll need to think creatively to combine these flavors in a harmonious and delicious way."

The camera panned to Ma and Vincenzo, who were eyeing each other warily from their cooking stations.

"Chefs, are you ready?" Rebecca asked.

"I born ready," Ma declared, tightening her apron.

Vincenzo puffed out his chest. "Mama Mia, let's-a get cooking!"

Rebecca turned back to the camera. "Alright, folks, the moment we've all been waiting for! Marieta, would you do the honors?"

Marieta stepped forward, her face serious. "Chefs, your challenge today is to create a dish that combines elements of Greek and Italian cuisine. I've given you a pantry full of several delicious ingredients and one very special one." She paused for dramatic effect. "And that secret ingredient is ... eel!"

A collective gasp went through the crowd as Marieta's assistants unveiled trays of fresh eel at each cooking station. Ma's eyes widened in surprise, while Vincenzo looked slightly pale. They both recovered quickly, straightening their aprons, ready to go.

"You have one hour to create your dish," Marieta continued. "Your dish should showcase your creativity and culinary skills while honoring both Greek and Italian traditions. And remember, presentation is key!"

Rebecca turned to the camera with an excited grin. "There you have it, folks! Our chefs will be battling it out with eel as their protein source. This is sure to be a slippery challenge! Chefs, your time starts ... now!"

With that, Ma and Vincenzo sprang into action. Ma immediately grabbed the eel, examining it closely before reaching for a sharp knife. Vincenzo hesitated for a moment, then dove for the pantry, pulling out an assortment of herbs and spices.

The kitchen became a flurry of activity as both chefs worked feverishly. The sizzle of pans and the rhythmic chopping of knives filled the air, along with the occasional Greek or Italian exclamation.

Ma seemed to be preparing some kind of eel stew,

her hands moving deftly as she chopped vegetables and added spices to a bubbling pot. The aroma of garlic and lemon began to fill the air.

Vincenzo, meanwhile, appeared to be going in a different direction. He was carefully filleting the eel and seemed to be preparing some kind of pasta dish. The smell of fresh basil and tomatoes mingled with the garlicky scent coming from Ma's station.

As the chefs worked, Rebecca moved among the spectators, gathering reactions.

"Jasper, as Ophelia's newest family member, how do you think your mother is doing so far?" Rebecca asked, holding the microphone out to Jasper.

Jasper grinned proudly. "Ma's in her element. She's got a few tricks up her sleeve that I bet will surprise everyone. And let me tell you, her eel stew smells amazing already."

Rebecca nodded, then turned to Maria Danza. "Maria, as a local business owner and baker, what do you think of this competition?"

Maria smiled brightly. "It's so exciting! Events like this really bring our community together. And I have to say, even though I'm Italian and a bit partial to Vinny, both dishes are smelling delicious. I can't wait to see what they come up with!"

As Rebecca continued to interview spectators, I watched Ma and Vincenzo intently. Despite their rivalry, both chefs seemed to be in their element, moving with confidence and precision.

Ma was now adding what looked like orzo to her stew, while Vincenzo was carefully layering thin slices of eel into what appeared to be a lasagna dish. The creativity on display was impressive.

Suddenly, there was a commotion near the entrance of *Aphrodite's*. I turned to see Evangeline Marinakis bursting through the doors, her face flushed and her eyes wild, as she waved her hands in the air.

"Stop!" she cried out, rushing towards the cooking stations, shaking her head over and over. "You can't do this!"

Security quickly moved to intercept her, but she dodged around them, making a beeline for Ma and Vincenzo.

"The eels!" Evangeline shouted. "They're not what you think!"

The room erupted into comments and speculations. Ma and Vincenzo froze at their stations, looking bewildered. Marieta stepped forward, her face a mask of confusion and concern.

"Ms. Marinakis, what is the meaning of this outburst?" Marieta demanded, clearly displeased with the interruption of her event.

Evangeline was breathing heavily, her eyes darting between the cooking stations and Marieta. "The eels!" Evangeline cried again, her voice shrill with panic. "They're not just any eels. They're from the church pond!"

A collective gasp went through the crowd. Ma dropped her spoon with a clatter, while Vincenzo took an instinctive step back from his cooking station.

Marieta stepped forward, her face a mix of irritation and anger. "Ms. Marinakis, I assure you these eels were sourced from a reputable supplier. They have nothing to do with the church."

"You're wrong!" Evangeline cried out, her eyes wild as she continued. "Those eels have been living in the sacred waters of the church pond for generations." Her eyes looked wild, almost crazed. "They're part of the legend! Using them like this ... it's sacrilege!"

The room overflowed with murmurs and exclamations. I exchanged a worried glance with Jaz, who had appeared at my side. I'd never heard of eels being part of the snake legend in Greece.

"Is this true?" Rebecca asked, turning to Marieta with her microphone extended.

Marieta's face paled slightly, but she quickly composed herself. "I assure you, there's been some misunderstanding. The eels used in this competition were sourced ethically and have no connection to the church or any legends. Frankly, I'm insulted by the accusations."

"Prove it," Evangeline said.

"I don't give away my sources." Marieta snapped her spine straight. "That would be culinary suicide."

But Evangeline wasn't backing down. "You're lying!" she shouted, pointing an accusing finger at Marieta. "I saw them being taken from the pond late last night. This is all part of some twisted plan!"

Security finally managed to restrain Evangeline, but the damage was done. The room was in an uproar, with spectators arguing amongst themselves and the camera crew frantically trying to capture every moment of the madness.

Ma and Vincenzo stood glued to their stations, looking helpless and worried. The dishes they'd been working on sat abandoned, steam still rising from the pots. Their faces revealed their thoughts, which happened to be in agreement for once: all that work for nothing.

The cookoff was officially over … no winner chosen.

〰

NIK AND BOOMER showed up to question Evangeline and Marieta. The chef was already on the phone with her attorneys, declaring Evangeline a quack out to ruin her reputation.

Pop and Jasper were doing their best to calm everyone down, while Jaz and I slipped out to get a firsthand look at the pond at the church.

"All these years of growing up here, and I never knew there were eels in this pond," I said to Oliver.

Oliver had agreed to meet us at the church. Sister had come out to join us shortly after we arrived. He and Sister Philothea had been doing research for his book on legends as well as helping Samuel look into the church's historical records.

"Well, it's not exactly common knowledge," Oliver replied, peering into the murky water of the church pond. "But eels can live in various environments, including ponds, but I've never heard them being part of the legend in Greece. Then again, the legend has never happened in the United States, so I supposed, anything is possible."

Sister Philothea nodded in agreement. "It doesn't surprise me that no one has seen them. They're quite elusive creatures. They tend to stay hidden in the depths of the pond."

Jaz crouched down by the water's edge, scanning the surface. "So how would someone even know they were here to take them?"

Oliver stroked his chin thoughtfully. "That's the question, isn't it? Only someone with intimate knowledge of the church's history and secrets would know about the eels existence."

I frowned, thinking back to Evangeline's outburst at *Aphrodite's*. "Evangeline seemed pretty certain about the eels being taken. Do you think she could have seen something?"

Sister Philothea shifted uncomfortably. "Evangeline seems a little obsessed with the church's traditions and the legend itself. Perhaps a bit too passionate at times. I fear for her mental health."

Oliver nodded in agreement. "She's so convinced about her speculations, she turns them into fact in her own mind without proper proof. But in this case, she may be onto something. The timing is certainly suspicious."

I crouched down next to Jaz, peering into the murky water. "Do you think we could actually see any eels from here?"

As if on cue, a dark, serpentine shape glided just beneath the surface before disappearing into the depths.

Jaz jumped back slightly. "Whoa! I guess that answers that question."

"Fascinating creatures, eels," Oliver mused. "Did you know they can live for decades? Some species even migrate thousands of miles to breed."

Sister Philothea cleared her throat. "While the eels are certainly interesting, I think we should focus on the more pressing matter at hand. If someone did take something—anything—it's a serious breach of the church's sacred grounds."

"Who would have the knowledge and access to do something like this?" I asked.

Oliver's eyes gleamed with excitement. "That's the real mystery, isn't it? We're dealing with someone who not only knows about the eels but also someone with vested interest in the church."

Jaz frowned. "But why? What's the motive behind taking the eels and using them in the cookoff?"

"Perhaps to scare people away," Sister Philothea suggested hesitantly. "So many people came to town to see the snakes, but after the snake attacks, people aren't so keen on touching them for good luck anymore. But they stuck around for the festival. Now that the festival is over, people stayed on to watch the cookoff. Planting snakes at local businesses and tying the eels to the legend and the church sound like more scare tactics to me. We've definitely lost more parishioners from all the bad luck"

I nodded in agreement. "You're right, Sister. Do you know if there are any security cameras around here that might have caught something?"

Sister Philothea shook her head. "Unfortunately, no. The church hasn't installed any cameras out of respect for the privacy of our parishioners."

"Convenient," Jaz muttered under her breath.

I shot her a warning glance before turning back to Sister Philothea and Oliver. "Has anyone else been asking about the eels recently? Or showing unusual interest in the pond? Or the grounds maybe?"

Oliver stroked his chin thoughtfully. "Now that you mention it, I did see Niles Turner hanging around."

I exchanged a meaningful glance with Jaz. "Niles Turner?"

Oliver nodded. "Yes. I spotted him near the pond a few days ago, looking rather intently at the water. At the time, I thought he was just another tourist fascinated by the famous legend appearing in the states for the first time ever. But now ..."

"Now it seems a bit more suspicious," Jaz finished for him.

Sister Philothea wrung her hands nervously. "I don't like to speak ill of anyone, but Mr. Turner has been asking a lot of questions about the church's history lately. More than your average visitor."

I frowned, thinking back to Niles' strange behavior and his visit to Nelson's jewelry store. "Did he ask anything specific about the eels or the pond?"

Sister Philothea hesitated before answering. "He ... he did inquire about any special properties the pond might have. I thought it was just curiosity about the legend, but now I'm not so sure."

I exchanged another meaningful glance with Jaz. This was starting to paint an interesting picture.

"Thank you both for your help," I said to Oliver and Sister Philothea. "You've given us a lot to think about."

As we prepared to leave, Oliver called out, "Oh, one more thing. I've been doing some additional research into the church's history, and I came across something rather intriguing about a unique looking snake key."

My spine tingled. No one was supposed to know about that. "What about it?"

Oliver's eyes gleamed with excitement. "Well, according to some old documents I found, there's not just one key, but three."

Jaz and I exchanged shocked looks.

"Oh, really? Wow. That's interesting. The question is, what do they unlock?" I asked.

"And that, my dear, is the mystery someone very clever might be able to crack." He gave me a knowing look.

My mind began to turn with endless possibilities ...

13

L ater that night, Nik and I sat out on our back deck, having a drink and watching the dogs play in the yard. Dark clouds had rolled in, so we were hoping the rain would hold off until the pups had enough exercise.

The weather coincided with the kind of day we'd had.

"Your ma was not happy about the *Hades' Kitchen Cookoff* disaster." Nik ran a hand through his thick, dark curls.

"I know. She kept blowing up my phone." I sipped my Chardonnay.

"Ophelia and Vinny both demanded a rematch, but *The Clearview Morning Show* was fully booked, and Marieta needed to move on to the next stop on her tour." Nik swirled the whisky in his glass.

"Ma said something about a compromise?"

Nik nodded. "Marieta declared them both winners since she never got to sample their dishes."

"That couldn't have gone over well. Where does the compromise come in?"

"Vinny took the prize money, and Ophelia settled on Marieta catering Jaz and Boomer's wedding."

My eyes sprang wide. "Seriously? I'm surprised Ma would let anyone cater the wedding other than her."

"She wants bragging rights to say a famous chef cooked in her kitchen, and Marieta agreed to sign a framed photo of them both for her to hang in the restaurant." Nik whistled to get Wolfgang's attention and shook his head for him to stop digging holes in the yard.

Wolf ignored Nik.

I clapped my hands, and Wolfy immediately stopped.

"I still don't know how you do that," Nik marveled. "I think he's more in love with you than he is me."

My heart melted. "Aww, he is a sweetie, when he's not slobbering on me. It took some time, but we've come to an understanding. I'll always love you more."

Nik winked, and my heart fluttered like it always did.

I thought about what he'd said about my mother. "That explains a lot about Ma," I said. "Marieta catering Jaz's wedding is a plus, I guess. Any publicity is good publicity for Ma's first baby, *Aphrodite's*. That would mean more than money any day."

"She's not wrong. That'll be quite the coup," Nik agreed. "Jaz and Boomer's wedding is in a few days. While Marieta might want to move on to the next stop on her tour, her lawyers are still battling the stolen eel accusation anyway, so she'll be here at least another week. That's why she agreed to Ophelia's compromise."

"Makes sense." I watched a bird swoop down and nearly get snatched by Prissy. "I'm sure Ma will insist on catering *our* wedding."

A shadow crossed over his face briefly, then it was

gone. "Well, that's a long way off. We don't have to worry about any of that yet."

Clearly his feet were still cold despite the muggy August weather.

"Speaking of eels, Jaz and I stopped by the church and spoke to Oliver and Sister Philothea."

Nik arched a brow at me. "Of course you did." He shook his head. "And what did the professor have to say?"

"He knew about the eels but had never heard of them being part of the legend. He did, however, enlighten us with fascinating details about the creepy creatures. And Sister said that Niles Turner had been asking a lot of questions and snooping around the pond lately."

"Marieta is adamant her eels are not from the church pond. It's really hard to tell if Evangeline's stories are true or figments of her imagination. She seems to be spiraling over this whole legend and snake infestation crisis. It doesn't help that she hasn't made any progress on declaring the church a historic monument, so the diocese is seriously considering cutting their losses and selling because of all the drama. Father is distraught. He doesn't want to start over in another town."

A rumble of thunder sounded off in the distance.

"We'd better bring in the pets before we find ourselves in another crisis." I glanced at the now black sky.

"Roger that." He headed for the dogs.

I grabbed Prissy and our glasses and headed inside.

He'd no sooner cleared the door than the sky opened up and rain began to pour.

I dried the dogs' feet when Nik's phone rang.

"Detective Stevens," he answered. "What? When?"
What now? was all I could think.

"I'll be right there." He hung up.

"What's wrong?"

"Nelson Rockwell just got bit by the poisonous snake while taking the trash out to the dumpster in the alley."

Nik and I secured the pets then rushed to the scene of Nelson Rockwell's snake bite. The rain had turned into a full-blown storm, and lightning flashed in the sky as we arrived at the back alley behind *Rockwell Jewelers.*

Nelson was lying on the ground, writhing in pain, while paramedics were tending to him. His hand was swollen and turning an alarming shade of red.

"Is he going to be okay?" I asked one of the paramedics.

"I don't know," he replied grimly as he worked on Nelson. "We need to get him to the hospital immediately."

Nik bent down beside a writhing Nelson and asked, "Do you know what kind of snake bit you?"

"It wasn't like the other kind. I worked at a zoo when I was younger. I ... I think it was a cottonmouth," Nelson gasped, shaking his head over and over. "I didn't see it coming ..."

My heart sank. There were two poisonous snakes on the loose now? Cottonmouths were known to be aggressive and deadly, especially if not treated immediately.

"Is there anything I can do?" I asked.

"Just check on Milly," he managed to get out.

"Don't worry, we'll take care of everything," Nik assured him before turning to me. "I'll handle this. You should probably go home and check on the babies. You know how Willow is afraid of thunder. And Wolfgang is a big baby over strong winds. Prissy is the only one who's probably okay."

"I'll call Milly on my way." I kissed his cheek and headed back to my car.

As I drove home through the heavy rain, my mind raced with thoughts about this latest incident. It seemed too coincidental that Nelson would get bitten by a snake on the night that Jaz and I had discovered new information about the church pond eels.

Clearly, whoever released the first snake wasn't done.

I checked in with Milly, who was an absolute mess. Luckily her mother lived close by and had gone over to watch her daughter so she could go to the hospital to be with Nelson. When I got home, I found Willow curled up in her bed, shaking from fear because of all the thunder booming outside.

Wolfgang was on the couch with his head buried beneath a pillow, and Prissy was nonchalantly cleaning herself from her perch way up high. I scooped up Willow and joined Wolfgang on the couch, crooning to them both until they calmed down before checking my phone for any updates from Nik.

Sure enough, there was a text from him saying that Nelson had been rushed into surgery due to complications from the snake bite. My stomach churned with worry for our friend and what his poor wife must be going through.

This truly was one of the worst days yet.

~

THE NEXT MORNING, Jaz and I met up at the police

station to speak with Nik and Boomer about the incident. They filled us in on the latest details.

"Nelson's condition is stable, but he's not out of the woods yet," Nik said, rubbing his tired eyes. "The doctors are optimistic, but it was a close call."

"Thank goodness." I sighed with relief.

"Have you been able to determine if it was definitely a cottonmouth?" Jaz asked, wringing her hands together.

Boomer nodded grimly, his face paling considerably. "The lab confirmed it based on the venom analysis. Which means we now have two highly venomous snakes on the loose in Clearview."

My cell phone rang. I answered it, "Hey, Jasper, what's up?"

"The mamas are missing."

"All of them?"

"Yes. And you know what that means ..."

"Oh, my Zeus, that can't be good." I noticed Nik and Boomer and even Jaz watching me like a hawk.

"Exactly! The whole town has heard about Nelson getting bit by the newest poisonous snake. You know the mamas ... they're always trying to save the day. Emily and I are going to stop by all their favorite places. You and Jaz patrol the streets."

Emily and Jasper? Maybe the mamas had been on to something. Speaking of mamas ... I really needed to put a tracker on Ma. She was making me gray, and I was only thirty. "I'm on my way." I hung up.

"What was that about, Ballas?" Nik narrowed his eyes.

"Kitchen crisis. All of the meat for tonight's special is spoiled." I shrugged. "They need me."

"I'll help," Jaz chimed in.

"Perfect." I grabbed her arm and headed for the door.

"Something smells fishy, but we've got bigger things to worry about right now," I heard Boomer say as we left the office.

"Okay, girl, spill it," Jaz said when we reached my car. "Where are we really going?"

"The mamas are missing."

Her eyes widened. "All of them?"

"Yes. And you know what that means ..."

"Trouble with a capital T."

"Jasper and Emily are looking at the places they love to go."

"Wait, Jasper and Emily? That's a thing?"

"Apparently so." I shrugged.

"So what's the plan?" she asked.

"You and I will drive down the streets in town. See if we spot them."

We drove around for what felt like an hour, not noticing anything out of the ordinary. Suddenly, I saw shadowed bodies in an alleyway several stores down from *Rockwell Jewelry Store*.

I slowed the car and pulled over. Jaz and I got out but kept to the shadows as we made our way down the alley. I couldn't believe the sight before me.

Ma, Aunt Tasoula, and Chloe wore snake print unitards and carried a long metal tool with a handle on one end that had a trigger and a gripping device on the other.

"Is that what Natalie was talking about? A snake grabber?" Jaz whispered from our hiding spot behind a trash can.

I squinted closer. I'd seen that before. "It looks like the grabber my papous used to pick things up when he had his total hip replacement." I shook my head.

"That's not nearly long enough to be a safe snake tong. What are they thinking?"

"Clearly they aren't." She chuckled. "Why the snake outfits? To look like even bigger snakes so the poisonous ones won't attack them?"

"Who knows, but clearly that's not logical." I texted Jasper where we found them, and he said they were on their way.

The mamas each carried a bucket with a lid and were currently looking under every piece of cardboard or trash surrounding the dumpster. A mouse ran out and Aunt Tasoula and Chloe started swinging their grabbers as they ran around in circles, fencing each other, screaming the entire time.

"Stop it, you nitwits," Ma snapped. "You gonna scare the snakes away." She picked up an empty to go coffee container. "People so lazy." She shook her head, her massive beehive swaying as she opened the dumpster and tossed the cup inside, then bent over to pick up more trash.

Everything happened at once.

A squirrel jumped out of the dumpster, over Ma's head, landing on Aunt Tasoula's chest. Aunt Tasoula screamed bloody murder, tossing the squirrel in the air. Chloe's grabber connected with the squirrel, Ma stood up ... and the squirrel sailed straight into Ma's beehive!

Jasper and Emily arrived just in time for the show.

Aunt Tasoula and Chloe swung at Ma's head like a piñata.

Ma bobbed and weaved while cursing in Greek.

Jasper ran to help.

And Emily went live for all her followers to see.

The pandemonium in the alley finally settled

down after Jasper managed to extract the terrified squirrel from Ma's beehive. The poor creature scampered away, likely traumatized for life. Ma's hair was a disaster, sticking out in all directions like she'd been electrocuted.

"Ma, what were you thinking?" Jasper scolded, hands on his hips. "You could have been seriously hurt!"

Ma huffed, trying to pat down her wild hair. "We thinking we catch dangerous snakes before they hurt more people! We heroes!"

"Heroes? More like fools," I muttered, stepping out from our hiding spot with Jaz. "You're lucky it was just a squirrel and not an actual venomous snake!"

The mamas had the decency to look sheepish as Emily continued to film the aftermath for her followers.

"Kalli! Jaz!" Ma exclaimed, her eyes widening. "What you doing here?"

"Saving you from yourselves, apparently," I replied, crossing my arms. "Do you have any idea how dangerous this is? Those snakes are deadly!"

Aunt Tasoula waved her hand dismissively. "Bah! We Greek women. We no afraid of little snakes."

"Little snakes?" Jaz echoed incredulously. "A cottonmouth nearly killed Nelson last night!"

The mamas exchanged guilty looks at that reminder.

"We just want to help," Chloe said softly. "This town is our home. We can't sit back and do nothing while people get hurt."

I felt my anger softening slightly at her words. Their hearts were in the right place, even if their methods were completely misguided.

I sighed, smoothing my hair back into its standard chignon, and counted to ten before responding. "I understand you want to help, but this isn't the way. You're putting yourselves in danger, and you could accidentally make things worse."

"She's right, Ma," Jasper added, his voice gentle but firm as he patted her back. "Let the professionals handle this. The best thing you can do is stay safe and keep an eye out for anything suspicious."

Ma opened her mouth to argue, but Aunt Tasoula put a hand on her arm. "Maybe they right, Ophelia. We no snake charmers."

"Speak for yourself," Chloe muttered, but she too looked resigned.

"Come on," I said, gesturing towards our cars. "Let's get you home before Nik and Boomer find out about this little adventure."

As we herded the mamas towards the vehicles, Emily finished up her livestream. "And there you have it, folks—another wild day in Clearview! Don't forget to like and subscribe for more small-town shenanigans!"

I blinked, suddenly realizing the odds of Nik and Boomer finding out were pretty good now that the Three Act Trio were celebrities.

Just then, my phone buzzed with a text from Nik: *Where are you? I stopped by Aphrodite's, but you weren't there.*

I showed the message to Jaz, who winced. "Oh, boy. You go," she said. "I'll make sure Aunt Tasoula and Chloe get home safely."

"Thanks," I replied gratefully. To Jasper, I added, "Can you and Emily take Ma home in your car? I need to go meet Nik."

Jasper nodded, already guiding Ma towards his vehicle.

I text Nik back: *Change of plans. Errands to run. Meet you at home. Explain later.*

14

Nik got called back to work on the case, so I stopped by the pet store on my way home. The familiar chime of the bell above the door greeted me as I stepped into *Paws, Whiskers & Claws* pet store. I inhaled deeply, the scent of animal feed and cedar shavings filling the air. A sense of calm washed over me as I grabbed a shopping basket and made my way towards the aisles dedicated to pet food.

As I perused the shelves, picking out cans of premium cat food for Ms. Priss and bags of kibble for Wolfgang and Willow, I noticed a flicker of movement out of the corner of my eye. I turned my head slightly and spotted Niles and Theo standing near the back of the store by the reptile section. My heart jumped into my throat.

What were they doing here?

I quickly ducked into the adjacent aisle, my heart pounding. Peeking through the gaps in the shelves, I strained to hear their conversation without being seen.

"You're not doing enough," Theo hissed, his voice low but urgent. "Time is running out. If we miss this opportunity, you get nothing."

Niles shifted, clearly agitated as he narrowed his eyes. He glanced around to make sure no one was listening before responding. "I'm working on another angle," he replied. "You need to be patient."

Theo's expression darkened. "It better be worth my while."

Niles' face hardened. "I could say the same thing, my friend. Careful who you're talking to. We might both be businessmen, but I'd say my associates are a bit, shall we say, more colorful than yours. You don't want to be on the wrong side of them."

I strained to catch every word. Just then, my elbow brushed against a stack of cans, sending them tumbling to the floor with a loud clatter. I froze, squeezing my eyes shut for a moment as my breath caught in my throat.

The sound had drawn their attention.

"What was that?" Niles said, his voice filled with suspicion.

I quickly picked up the cans, my hands trembling. Before I could hide, Niles and Theo rounded the corner and saw me.

"Kalli Ballas," Niles said, a forced smile spreading across his face. "Fancy seeing you here."

I plastered a smile on my face, trying to appear nonchalant. "Oh, hey, Niles. Theo. Just getting some food for my pets. What brings you two to *Paws, Whiskers & Claws*?"

"Picking up some food for my bird," Theo answered.

"In the reptile section?" The words escaped my mouth before I could bite them back. I pressed my lips together to keep from saying anything else.

Theo smirked, his eyes narrowing slightly. "Just

browsing. You know how it is. Always on the lookout for a new addition."

I nodded, pretending to be engrossed in reading labels and rearranging the cans. "Sure, sure. You and Niles have gotten pretty chummy since he arrived in town. Did you know each other before?" I glanced up at him.

"Niles here was tagging along. He's interested in maybe buying a property for a new business venture."

"Oh, nice. What kind of business?" I turned my attention on Niles. "How's everything going?"

Niles crossed his arms, his expression guarded. "Fine. Everything's fine. You sure do ask a lot of questions."

"I *am* a business owner, so I'm curious about other businesses in town. And, well, my fiancé *is* a detective after all. I guess he's rubbing off on me." I laughed a little too shrilly then swallowed hard.

"When I iron out all the details with Theo, I'll be sure to let you know." Niles leveled a pointed look at Theo.

I could sense the tension between them. Something was definitely up. "That's good to hear. We love to support fellow businesses around here," I said, trying to sound casual. "If I can help in any way, just let me know."

"Much appreciated, Ms. Ballas." Niles' was charming but hard to read.

"You know, with everything happening in Clearview lately, it's important to stay vigilant. The streets are dangerous, especially with a killer on the loose." Theo's smirk widened, but there was no humor in his eyes. "So, you be careful out there, Kalli."

I didn't like the way his words sounded like a

veiled threat. "Thanks for the advice. I'll be sure to do that. Same to you both."

They exchanged a glance before turning and walking away, leaving me standing there, feeling oddly creeped out. I watched them leave the store, a sense of unease settling in the pit of my stomach. Whatever they were involved in, it was clear that it was something serious. And now I was more determined than ever to find out what it was.

Gathering my purchases, I made my way to the checkout, my mind humming with possibilities. I knew I had to be careful looking into men like them, but I couldn't shake the feeling that something big was about to happen in Clearview.

And I needed to be ready.

As I drove home, the evening sky was painted in hues of orange and pink. I couldn't help but replay the encounter in my head. What could Theo and Niles be plotting? Did it have to do with the church land Theo wanted? Or maybe they were the ones who had released the poisonous snakes. Why else would they be in the reptile section of a pet store?

Did Niles kill his wife Sigrid?

The weight of their secret pressed down on me, fueling my determination to uncover the truth. When I got home, I sat at my kitchen table, a cup of tea steaming beside me. I pored over my notes on the investigation into Sigrid's death, the poisonous snake attacks, and the suspicions regarding the legend of the snakes and the church.

I felt like we were running in circles, getting nowhere.

Bjorn's name still wasn't cleared as he was the last person with Sigrid, knew about snakes, and had no alibi. Nik would never set a wedding date while worrying about clearing his father's name. He and Boomer were working late, trying to solve this case with the mayor breathing down the captain's neck for answers.

So, I fed the pets and went to bed feeling troubled.

THE NEXT MORNING, I decided to take a different route on my usual walk with the dogs, passing by Theo's house. It was a modest place, with a neatly kept garden and a white picket fence. I slowed down, pretending to tie my shoelace, while discreetly observing. A black car was parked outside, and I could see shadows moving behind the curtains. Suddenly, the shadows stopped and the curtains parted.

I quickly stood and kept walking, not looking back.

It didn't take me long to get home and settle the dogs, then I changed and met Jaz at our favorite bakery, *Sinfully Delicious*. Over coffee, tea, and pastries, I filled her in on the strange encounter at the pet store and then this morning's walk.

Jaz, ever the skeptic, raised an eyebrow. "I knew Niles and Theo must be working on something together, but you really think Niles is buying a business in Clearview? It's such a small town compared to the business he owns in New York City."

"I don't know for sure," I admitted, "but my instincts are screaming that story is just a cover for what they're really involved in."

Jaz stirred her cappuccino thoughtfully. "Maybe they were looking for something in the reptile section to lure more eels out of the church pond. It's still weird how he's been hanging around the church asking all those questions about its history."

I nodded. "I agree." I finished my tea.

"Hey, I wonder if Thalia has found out anything more on the whole clause in the deed regarding the Blackheart family regaining rights to the land if the church goes under." Jaz finished her pastry.

"The last time Nik talked to her, she said the church was having financial problems." I shrugged. "But that's not out of the norm with most parishes. The snake infestation certainly hasn't helped."

"Maybe it's time you paid a visit to Thalia yourself." Jaz threw our trash away. "I'm going across the street to open up for the day. I'll cover for you if anyone stops in and needs anything from you."

"Thanks, Jaz. You're a life saver. If anyone can help, Thalia can."

~

THE BELL above the door chimed softly as I stepped into Thalia's law office, a small yet welcoming space adorned with shelves of legal tomes and family photographs. The scent of fresh flowers from the vase on her desk mingled with the faint aroma of coffee. Thalia looked up from her paperwork, her eyes lighting up with a warm smile.

"Kalli! What brings you here today?" she asked, standing to give me a quick hug.

"Hey, Thalia," I replied, returning her embrace. "I wanted to see if you've found any more information about the clause in the deed for the church property records."

I knew she couldn't talk about the church's finances or any legal issues she was handling for Father; however, she was helping Nik with the investigation, and she knew I was a consultant. So, she should be able to share issues related to the case.

Thalia motioned for me to sit in the chair across from her desk and resumed her seat. Her expression turned serious. "You mean the clause regarding the Blackheart family's rights to the land if the church ceases to operate as a place of worship?"

"Exactly," I nodded. "You mentioned that an English merchant named Reginald Blackheart donated the land to the Greek Orthodox Church back in the late 1800s, even though he wasn't Greek himself."

Thalia sighed, tapping her pen thoughtfully against the desk. "Yes, that's right. The clause states that if the church closes, the land reverts back to the descendants of the original donor. With the snake infestation slowing down, tourists leaving town because of two poisonous snakes on the loose, and the loss of parishioners because of the 'bad luck', there's a real risk of the church shutting down. If that happens, a Blackheart descendant could claim the land."

I folded my hands so I wouldn't fidget. "Have you found any living Blackheart heirs?"

Thalia shook her head. "Not yet. It's been challenging, but I'm working on it. However, I did come across something new that might challenge the claim if it comes up."

My eyes widened. "What did you find?"

"There's a possibility that the clause could be contested due to some irregularities in the original documentation," Thalia explained. "For instance, there are discrepancies in the signatures on the deed and some missing seals that were supposed to authenticate the transfer of the land. Moreover, Reginald Blackheart's donation was made under somewhat unclear circumstances, and there are hints that the documentation might not have been properly validated by the authorities at the time. I'm still digging into it, but if I can prove these issues, we might be able to nullify the clause altogether as invalid and the land would stay with the church."

I exhaled in relief. "That's good to hear."

"The diocese could still decide to sell if the church doesn't recover financially."

"What about Father Papadopoulos? How's he holding up?"

Thalia's eyes softened with concern. "I can't talk specifics, but in general, he's doing his best to keep the church afloat, but it's tough. As you know, that snake of a human being, Theo, is circling like a vulture, waiting for any opportunity to claim the land if Father can't keep the church operating and the diocese decides to sell. I'm doing everything I can to help Father, legally speaking."

"Thank you, Thalia," I said earnestly. "It means a lot to the community and to me personally."

Thalia smiled. "Of course, Kalli. I'm glad to help." She leaned back in her chair, a playful glint in her eye. "So, how's the wedding planning going?"

I couldn't help but roll my eyes. "Well, Nik's been stalling on setting a wedding date. I think he's got cold feet."

Thalia reached across the desk to pat my hand. "Nik's just got a lot on his plate right now. He adores you. You know that."

I sighed, feeling the weight of the situation. "I know it's a lot for him, but it's hard not to feel like he's avoiding the wedding altogether. I'm usually the one dragging my feet. It really has me rattled that he's hesitating now."

"Well, don't forget," Thalia continued, "Aunt Chloe accepting the captain's marriage proposal just to get back at Uncle Bjorn isn't helping. At least Bjorn has backed off on pursuing her. It's a mess, but Nik loves you. He just needs time to sort things out."

"Thanks, Thalia," I said, appreciating her reassurance. "I needed to hear that."

Thalia chuckled. "You're welcome. At least you're engaged." She huffed out a breath and shook her head.

"Speaking of relationships, let's talk about you." I studied her with concern. "How are things going with Parker?"

Thalia's expression had turned from playful to frustrated. "Honestly, it's been tough. I know he's busy as a senator, but I'm busy, too, as a lawyer. All the more reason to make the most of our time together. He hasn't asked me to move in with him yet, and I'm starting to think he's in no rush to take the next step forward. I don't know how much longer I'm willing to wait around for him."

I shook my head sympathetically. "That sounds frustrating. Have you talked to him about it?"

"I have," she admitted, "but he always says the timing isn't right. I'm beginning to wonder if it ever will be."

"We should hang out soon," I suggested, hoping to lift her spirits. "Maybe a girls' night out at *Flannigan's Pub* to take our minds off things? Actually, Jaz loves it there. Maybe we'll do her bachelorette party there. I'll plan it and give you the details soon."

Thalia's face brightened. "That sounds like a great idea. Just say when, and I'll be there. Thanks, Kalli."

As I stood to leave, I felt a sense of camaraderie and support that only deepened my gratitude for Thalia. "You're welcome, and thank you for everything, Thalia. I'll keep you updated on any developments."

"Anytime, Kalli," she replied with a smile. "Take care and let me know if you need anything."

I left Thalia's office feeling a mix of relief and renewed determination. As I stepped outside, my phone buzzed with a tip from one of my contacts. Ma might have her Greek phone tree ... but I had my Greek tip tree. I always had eyes and ears on all things happening in Clearview.

Something was going down in the warehouse section of town right now.

I thought of texting Nik, but I knew he had meetings all day today, and there was no time to lose. I had to check it out.

The streets leading to the warehouse district were eerily quiet, which was odd since it was midday. The sun was high in the sky, casting long shadows that danced across the pavement. I approached the area cautiously, wondering if I'd made a mistake going alone. Maybe I should have called Jaz and had her meet me on her lunch break. The tip had mentioned unusual activity, and I couldn't shake the feeling that this could be connected to Theo and Niles' mysterious dealings.

I parked down the street and crept through the darkened alleys, my senses on high alert. The largest warehouse loomed ahead, its rusted doors slightly ajar. Peeking inside, my breath caught at the sight of Theo and Niles in a heated discussion with a group of men. The atmosphere was tense, and I could sense the danger radiating from the gathering. There was a large delivery truck with no insignia on the side parked just behind them.

My mind raced with questions. What were they planning? What was their endgame? And how did this all tie back to the church and the land?

Determined to uncover the truth, I decided to stay hidden and observe. This was my chance to gather crucial information and piece together the puzzle that had been haunting Clearview. As I watched from the shadows, I knew that every moment counted, and the stakes had never been higher.

The conversation inside the warehouse grew more animated, and I strained to hear snippets of their discussion. Words like "property," "deal," and "deadline" floated through the air, fueling my suspicions. It was clear that whatever they were planning, it was happening soon, and it could have devastating consequences for our community.

I glanced at my watch, noting the time. I would share this information with Nik later, but first, I needed to gather as much evidence as I could. Carefully, I pulled out my phone and began recording the scene, capturing the faces, voices, and the tension that filled the warehouse. This evidence could make all the difference in our fight to protect the church, our heritage, and our town.

As I continued to record, I couldn't help but think about Nik and our future. After renewing my determination from talking to Thalia, I now felt a renewed sense of purpose and resolve. We would get through this, together, and come out stronger on the other side.

It was what we did.

With the recording safely stored on my phone, I slipped away from the warehouse, my mind already racing with plans. There was still so much to do, but I knew that with Thalia's legal expertise, Father Papadopoulos's unwavering faith, and the support of my friends and family, we could stand against any threat that came our way.

It was the Greek way.

As I made my way to *Full Disclosure*, I felt a surge of adrenaline. This fight was far from over. I needed more evidence. I would find a time when no one was there and come back. And this time I wasn't leaving until I found something worth looking for.

15

As the sun dipped below the horizon, casting long shadows over Clearview, I knew it was time. Nik's meetings ran late, so I convinced Jaz to come with me. We parked down the street again and walked. The town was silent, wrapped in darkness, with only the occasional streetlamp flickering in the distance.

Jaz and I stood a ways away, staring at the old warehouse, a hulking mass of rusted metal and broken windows. The night air was cold, smelling of damp earth and salt from the river that ran behind the building. Every now and then, a gust of wind rattled a loose sheet of metal somewhere in the structure, making it groan like something alive.

Jaz pulled her hoodie tighter around her. "You do realize this is the part in horror movies where the dumb characters get themselves killed, right?"

I pulled my jacket tighter around me, feeling a mix of anticipation and trepidation. "Good thing we're not dumb, then."

She rolled her eyes, but there was a hint of nervousness in her posture as she scanned the darkened lot around us. We both suspected this place had been cleared out earlier, but there was always a chance someone had stuck around.

"Ready for this?" Jaz's voice broke through my thoughts, her eyes bright with curiosity and nervous excitement.

"More than ever," I replied, my voice steady despite the nervous flutter in my stomach. "We need to find out what they're hiding, and tonight's our best shot."

Together, we made our way slowly to the warehouse door.

The structure loomed dark and foreboding against the twilight sky. The building was old, its wooden beams creaking with age, and the smell of damp wood and musty air filled my nostrils. The gravel crunched beneath our feet as we approached, each step echoing in the stillness of the night.

"Stay close," I whispered, glancing around to ensure we were alone.

The silence was almost oppressive, broken only by the distant hoot of an owl and the soft chirping of crickets. I slipped on a pair of gloves and tried the side door first—locked, of course. But I already had a backup plan. Moving to the back, I climbed up onto a rusted old dumpster, balancing carefully before reaching up to the broken window I found last time.

Having second thoughts about germs, I looked down at Jaz pleadingly. "Want to switch places and go first?"

"This one is all you, girl."

I sighed, then whispered, "Well, I can't reach it, so you're going to have to climb up here and help boost me up."

Jaz grumbled as she scrambled onto the dumpster beside me, then laced her fingers together and crouched. "If I get tetanus from this, I'm making you pay for my medical bills."

I stepped into her hands and hoisted myself up, gripping the windowsill. The jagged glass was long gone, leaving only rough metal edges, which I avoided as I wriggled through. I could only imagine what rust could do to my insides.

My boots hit the concrete floor with a soft thud. A second later, Jaz followed, landing next to me. We were immediately enveloped in darkness. I pulled out my phone and switched on the flashlight, the beam cutting through the gloom.

Inside, the warehouse was eerily quiet. Dust hung in the air, illuminated by the thin slivers of moonlight that seeped through the high, broken skylights. The space smelled of oil, mildew, and something faintly metallic. Rusted machinery sat abandoned in the corners, covered in cobwebs.

The only sound in the room was our cautious footsteps and the occasional drip of water from the ceiling. The air was thick with dust, making me want to sneeze. We moved carefully, our eyes scanning the room for any signs of evidence.

"Alright," Jaz whispered, rubbing her arms. "What exactly are we looking for?"

"Anything. Documents, hidden compartments, maybe some clue about what they were doing here. Look for anything that seems out of place," I instructed Jaz, my voice barely above a whisper. "We need clues, anything that might tell us what they're planning."

We spread out, moving cautiously.

My fingers brushed against an old worktable, the wood rough and splintered beneath my touch. I checked inside a few drawers—nothing but old tools and empty cans. Jaz kicked at a discarded box, but it was filled with nothing but dust and crumpled paper.

After twenty minutes, we found exactly nothing.

Jaz exhaled, frustrated. "So, this was a waste of time?"

Frustration began to gnaw at me, but I pushed it aside, determined to remain focused. "Just keep looking. There has to be something we're missing."

It was then that Jaz stumbled upon something.

"Hey, Kalli, check this out," she called softly, pointing to a slightly raised section of the floorboards.

My heart skipped a beat as I crouched beside her, running my fingers over the wood. It felt different, almost hollow. "Help me lift this," I said.

Together we pried the floorboard open, revealing a trap door beneath. A rush of cold air hit us, carrying with it a musty, earthy scent.

"An underground tunnel," I breathed, my eyes wide and wary. "Do you think it could lead us to more answers?"

"Only one way to find out," she replied.

I was already shaking my head. "That's a hard no from me."

She pulled out her phone and shined the light down. A stone staircase descended into darkness. "C'-mon. Aren't you the least bit curious?"

I groaned but followed her as I carefully stepped down. This was such a bad idea.

The air grew cooler as we traveled lower, the sound of our breathing echoing off the ancient stone walls. When we reached the bottom, the tunnel stretched ahead of us, barely wide enough for two people to walk side by side. The walls were rough, carved from old stone, damp with age. Roots dangled from the ceiling, and the floor was uneven, covered in dirt and small puddles.

Our phone flashlights were our only guide through the narrow, damp tunnel.

"This place must be ancient," I murmured, marveling at the age of the structure. "I wonder how long it's been here."

"This feels way older than the warehouse," Jaz said, sweeping her phone light along the wall. "Like centuries-old." She looked around in awe.

I nodded, my heart pounding. "Who built this? And more importantly—why?"

As we ventured deeper, the tunnel branched out into different directions. We paused, considering our options.

"Which way?" Jaz asked, her voice echoing softly.

"Let's try the left path first," I suggested, and we moved forward, our footsteps echoing in the confined space. The tunnel seemed to stretch on forever, and just as we began to doubt our choice, we emerged into the woods.

The night was pitch-black, the towering trees casting long, eerie shadows that danced in the moonlight. The sounds of the forest surrounded us—the rustling of leaves, the distant howl of a wolf. It was disorienting, and I could feel the unease settling in on the verge of a panic attack.

"We can't risk getting lost out here," I said, my voice tight with worry. "Let's head back and try another tunnel."

We retraced our steps, the tunnel seeming even more oppressive than before. At the junction, we chose a different path, this time moving with greater caution. The tunnel twisted and turned, the walls closing in around us. I could feel my heart pounding in my chest, each beat echoing in the silence.

Suddenly, we heard voices. Male voices, deep and gruff, reverberating through the tunnel. One of them sounded eerily familiar.

"Quick, this way!" I urged, pulling Jaz along another path. We moved swiftly, the voices growing fainter until they were just a distant murmur. The tunnel finally led us to an exit, and we found ourselves in an alleyway behind the library, which was as old as the church.

Breathing a sigh of relief, I turned to Jaz. "That voice ... it sounded like Dale, the church's groundskeeper. Why would he be down there?"

"I don't know," Jaz replied, shaking her head. "But it means we're onto something. I wonder if he's involved in something with Theo and Niles? We need to figure what he's involved in for sure and why."

"We will," I promised, feeling a sense of pride over conquering my fear and a sense of accomplishment. "But for now, let's get out of here before we're spotted."

We slipped through the alley, our senses heightened as we made the long trek back to our car. The night was still, the town seemingly unaware of the secrets lurking beneath its surface. As we drove home, I couldn't shake the feeling that we were on the brink of uncovering something much bigger than we had ever imagined.

∼

THE DAWN BROKE with a sense of urgency. Nik and Boomer were still so busy dealing with the poisonous snakes on the loose and their ongoing investigation of

Sigrid's murder that we barely saw either of them. I would fill them in on what we found when we knew more. After tending to our pets, I headed to the library to meet Jaz.

The ancient building stood tall and imposing, its stone facade weathered by time. Inside, the smell of old books and polished wood greeted us, a comforting reminder of the knowledge contained within.

We split up to cover more ground, searching through archives, old maps, and historical records. Hours passed in silence, broken only by the occasional rustle of pages. Finally, Jaz called me over, her eyes wide with excitement.

"Look at this," she said, pointing to a map dated back to the 1800s. "It shows the tunnel system beneath Clearview, including the warehouse and the church. And this says it was originally used during times of war or territorial disputes to hide troops, store supplies and communicate in secret, but it was later condemned and no longer used."

My heart raced as I studied the map, realizing just how extensive the network was. "I'd say someone is definitely using it again for lord only knows what based on the voices we overheard," I whispered. "This is it. This could be the key to everything."

Armed with this new information, we knew our next steps were critical. We had to tell Nik and Boomer.

Knowing our men, we decided to soften the news with food from *Aphrodite's*, hoping they wouldn't be mad. Making a quick stop by my parents' restaurant, we picked up our orders and surprised the guys with lunch.

Nik and Boomer stared at us in disbelief, eating their gyros, as Jaz and I finished recounting our discovery of the underground tunnels. We were huddled in Nik's office at the police station, the blinds drawn to ensure privacy.

"Let me get this straight," Nik said, pinching the bridge of his nose. "You two broke into an abandoned warehouse, found a secret tunnel system, and overheard suspicious voices that might include Dale, the church groundskeeper?"

I nodded, trying not to squirm under his intense gaze. "I know it sounds crazy, but it's all true. We have the map to prove it." I spread out the old map we'd found at the library on Nik's desk.

Boomer leaned in, studying the intricate network of tunnels. "This is ... incredible. And potentially very dangerous." He leveled Jaz with a stern look.

"You two were busy with your own investigation," Jaz said, "and you both agreed that people tend to talk to us."

"Talking to people, I'm okay with," Boomer said. "Spying on questionable characters in old warehouses and traipsing through ancient, condemned tunnels, not so much."

She shrugged. "We were just trying to help."

Nik looked at me, his expression a mix of concern and resolve. "We need to investigate this further, but we can't do it alone. It's too risky."

Boomer nodded in agreement. "We'll assemble a team to explore these tunnels. If Dale is involved, we need to find out what he's up to and why."

A sense of relief washed over me, knowing we wouldn't be facing this danger alone. "Thank you," I said sincerely. "We'll help in any way we can."

"Preferably from the sidelines," Nik added.

Jaz gave me a knowing look. There were plenty of other things we could do from the *sidelines*.

"You need to be cautious," I said. "Whoever is using these tunnels has to be desperate. They look ready to cave in."

Nik gave a curt nod. "We'll proceed carefully. For now, you two should stay away and let us handle the investigation. We'll keep you updated. If you heard them, they might have heard or seen you. It's not worth the risk."

Reluctantly, we agreed. Nik and Boomer began strategizing as Jaz and I left the police station. Outside, the sun was high in the sky, casting a warm glow over the town. We walked in silence, both lost in our thoughts.

Finally, she broke the silence. "This is bigger than we thought, isn't it?"

I nodded, my mind racing with possibilities. "I wonder if this is what Samuel was talking about."

"I wonder just how much Father knows," she replied.

"That is the biggest question yet," I muttered.

Jaz continued with concern etched on her face. "Do you think he's been keeping things from you and Nik?"

I sighed. "It's possible. He has always been secretive, but this ... this feels different." I frowned. "We need to find out the truth. If Father knows something, we have to confront him. It's the only way we can help Nik and Boomer effectively."

"Agreed, but my wedding is right around the corner, and *we* have a ton to do, still, Ms. Maid of Honor." She crossed her arms and looked at me with a raised brow.

"You're right. You've done so much to help me with this case to clear Bjorn's name. The guys can handle it. It's time we put you first, and I have the perfect place for your bachelorette party. I really am so excited for you."

"Thank you." She hugged me quickly. *Don't worry, your day will come soon.*

I smiled my appreciation at her, but I wasn't so sure about that.

16

I stood outside the barn, my heart swelling with anticipation and joy. Jaz's bachelorette party at *Flannigan's Pub* with the girls had been perfect. Then, true to my word, I had spent every last minute finalizing the details for her big day.

And now the day was here!

The rustic charm of the venue was undeniable—sunlight filtered through the wooden slats, casting a warm glow over the hay bales and wildflower arrangements. The air was filled with the sweet scent of blooming lavender and freshly cut grass, mingling with the mouthwatering aroma of Marieta Galanis's culinary masterpieces being prepared inside the barn. The distant murmur of conversation and laughter reached my ears, blending with the soft chirping of birds and the rustling of leaves in the gentle breeze.

Jaz, my best friend, emerged from the bridal suite, looking radiant and ethereal in her flowing white gown. Her eyes sparkled with excitement, and her smile was contagious. "Kalli, I can't believe this day is finally here!" she exclaimed, her voice trembling with emotion.

I hugged her tightly, feeling a lump form in my

throat. "You look absolutely stunning, Jaz. Boomer is one lucky man," I said, trying to keep my voice steady.

She laughed, a melodious sound that always lifted my spirits. "Thank you, but I couldn't have done any of this without you. You've been my rock through all the craziness."

"Hey, what are best friends for?" I replied, giving her hand a reassuring squeeze.

As we made our way to the ceremony area inside the barn, I marveled at how beautifully everything had come together. The wooden beams were adorned with twinkling fairy lights, and Marieta's delectable creations were arranged on long tables covered in crisp white linens.

The scent of roasted lamb, garlic, and herbs made my stomach rumble, and I couldn't help but admire the skill and artistry that went into each dish. Despite the controversy surrounding her, Marieta had out-done herself.

Detective Nik Stevens, my gorgeous fiancé, stood at the front of the barn, his handsome face reflecting the pride and love he felt for his best friend, Boomer. He wore a simple yet elegant suit and a white rose bou-tonniere. I felt a surge of affection for him as he caught my eye and winked. He had gotten ordained specifi-cally for this occasion, and I knew how much it meant to him to officiate Jaz and Boomer's wedding.

The ceremony began, and I watched with tears in my eyes as Jaz walked down the aisle on the arm of her father. Boomer's face lit up with pure joy as he gazed at his bride. Nik's voice was steady and warm as he led them through their vows, and the love and commitment between Jaz and Boomer were palpable. When they finally kissed, sealing their promises to each other, the barn erupted in cheers and applause.

The reception that followed was a whirlwind of laughter, music, and celebration. The Greek mamas were in full festive mode, toasting with ouzo and shouting "Opa!" at every opportunity, even though Jaz and Boomer weren't Greek.

The band played a variety of music to satisfy all their guests, and the dance floor was never empty. The first dance between Jaz and Boomer was magical, their movements synchronized and graceful, as if they were the only two people in the world.

I took a deep breath before giving my maid of honor speech, my heart pounding in my chest. "Ladies and gentlemen, I've known Jaz since we were kids, and seeing her so happy today fills me with joy. Boomer, you've found yourself a gem, and I know you'll cherish her for the rest of your lives together. Let's raise our glasses to love, friendship, and the beautiful journey ahead. To Jaz and Boomer!" The crowd cheered, and I felt a warm glow of happiness as I clinked glasses with Jaz.

Nik's best man speech was equally touching, filled with heartfelt anecdotes and humor. He spoke of Boomer's dedication and bravery as a detective, and how lucky he was to have found someone as wonderful as Jaz. The guests laughed and cried, and I saw the deep bond between Nik and Boomer reflected in every word.

As the night wore on, the festivities continued with throwing the bouquet. Jaz's bouquet sailed through the air, and to everyone's delight, Nik's Ma Chloe caught it. She beamed with happiness at Captain Quincy Crenshaw, even though her ex-husband Bjorn was present, and the crowd erupted in applause.

There was a sense of excitement and anticipation in the air, and I felt peace and contentment knowing I was engaged to Nik. The entire evening was a welcome relief from the ongoing investigations of murder, legends, secret tunnels, and more. For a little while, our troubles were gone.

I should have known that was too good to be true.

Suddenly, chaos broke out when tiny garden snakes appeared everywhere in the barn.

The Greek mamas shrieked and jumped onto the tables, chanting prayers and making the sign of the cross. The guests scattered in all directions, trying to avoid the slithering creatures. As Jasper's plus one, Emily, the travel blogger, seized the moment and went live on her phone, capturing the pandemonium for her followers.

Jaz's parents stood in the middle of the chaos, their eyes wide with horror.

Nik and Boomer quickly took charge, guiding the guests outside while we waited for Natalie and her team to arrive and the snakes to be safely removed. Marieta, ever the professional, continued to serve her delicious dishes, unperturbed by the unexpected turn of events.

As the night drew to a close, the barn finally snake-free, I found myself standing with Nik under the twinkling fairy lights. He wrapped his arms around me, pulling me close. "Well, that was certainly a memorable wedding," he said, his voice filled with weariness.

I rested my head on his shoulder. "Definitely one for the books. But despite everything, it was perfect. Jaz and Boomer are so happy, and that's all that matters." I paused a beat and then asked the question that had been plaguing me lately. "Are you happy?"

"Of course I am, Ballas." Nik kissed the top of my head, and I felt a sense of contentment wash over me.

"We'll have our special day soon, Kalli. I promise. I just ... can't think about that right now until my father's name is cleared and the murder solved." *Please tell me you're okay with that?*

I nodded and smiled, feeling hopeful for the future.

As the music played softly in the background and the stars shone brightly above, I knew that no matter what challenges lay ahead, we would be fine. I had to believe that everything would work with us because we were meant to be together.

He was my person.

As we said our goodbyes and the guests began to leave, I took one last look at the barn, now quiet and serene. The memories of this day would stay with me forever, a testament to the power of love, friendship, and resilience. And as I walked hand in hand with Nik, I couldn't help but wonder what our wedding might look like ...

And what trouble might be headed our way.

THE DAY HAD BARELY dawned when I received a call that set the tone for what would be an unforgettable adventure. It was Aunt Tasoula, her voice brimming with excitement and a hint of mischief.

"Kalliope, we have plan. Meet us at old town square."

I knew better than to question the Greek mamas, especially when Aunt Tasoula, Ma, and Chloe put their heads together. They were a formidable trio, always ready to tackle any challenge with the tenacity and spirit of true warriors.

That required in-person supervision.

As I arrived at the town square, I couldn't help but burst into laughter. There they were, dressed in camo outfits complete with warpaint streaks on their faces, ready to blend in with the bushes. They looked like they were prepared to take on an army, not catch snakes.

"Kalli, you just in time!" Ma called out as she adjusted her headband, her beehive sitting high above. "We gonna set traps over town. We catch pesky snakes for all."

"We use Greek food as bait," Aunt Tasoula added with a wink. "Who no like Greek food, right?"

"We gonna win this time." Chloe raised her fist in the air.

I shook my head, amused but impressed by their determination. No way would I let them do this, but I couldn't resist hearing their plan. "Alright, what's the plan?"

The mamas laid out their strategy with military precision. They were gonna prepare a variety of traps, each filled with delectable Greek dishes like spanakopita, souvlaki, and baklava. The idea was to lure the snakes with the irresistible aroma of our traditional food.

I didn't have the heart to tell them they would prefer rodents.

"Ma, the answer is no." I crossed my arms and shook my head. "You can't be serious. After the snake charming disaster, and the snake tong fiasco, what makes you think snake traps will be any better?"

"You say no be sneaky sneaky, so I tell you." She threw up her hands. "Now you say you no help. You waste our time." She started to walk away, and the other mamas followed.

"You're right, I'm not going to help you do something else to put yourselves in danger." I followed them. "I need to get to work. Please tell me you're going home."

"We go home," they all said in unison.

That was too easy.

"I mean it. The police don't need anything else to worry about."

They waved me off, ignoring me. I gave up and headed into work, but this time I called Jasper and gave him the heads up to be on the lookout for the mamas.

"You won't believe what the mamas are up to this time," I said to Jaz when I reached *Full Disclosure*.

Jaz and Boomer had decided to wait on their honeymoon until after the investigation was over with. Boomer didn't feel right leaving Nik to clear his father's name alone.

Jaz groaned. "What now?"

"Snake trapping." I sighed. "Snake charming and snake catching didn't work, so they figure trapping is the way to go. I told them to go home."

"They have no idea what they're doing. You would think poisonous snakes and squirrel attacks would have scared them enough to make them stay out of this."

"We're talking about Greek mamas here. Protecting their families at any cost is what they do."

"Do you think they'll listen to you this time?" She finished getting the register ready and then turned the open sign on.

"I hope so, but somehow I doubt it." I headed for my loft. "Let me know if anyone needs me. I'm putting the finishing touches on your outfits for your honeymoon."

"Will do, and yay! I can't wait to see them. Holler if you need anything."

I nodded and then disappeared upstairs to get to work. It didn't take long for the phone call I was dreading to come.

I answered my cell phone. "Hi, Nik. What's up?"

"Our phones are ringing off the hook with calls coming in about traps going off all over town. Do you know anything about this?"

"The mamas are snake trapping this time," I reluctantly responded.

"Why didn't you tell me what they were up to?" I could hear the exhaustion and frustration in his tone.

"Because I knew you guys were busy with the case. I'm sorry, Nik. This is exactly what I was trying to avoid. I told them to go home."

"Well, apparently, they didn't listen to you." His tone sounded sharper than normal. There was a pause on the line. "I'm sorry. I'm not mad at you. I'm just distracted and worried about my father. We really don't have time for this."

"I know. Maybe we can help. Where are you going?"

"The park."

"We'll meet you there." I hung up, told Jaz what had happened, and we headed out after our assistants got there to cover the store.

Our first stop was Clearview Park. It didn't take long to find the trap. Just follow the crowd gathered in a circle. We approached the trap cautiously, expecting to find a snake. Instead, we found a fluffy dog wagging its tail and sniffing at the remnants of a souvlaki stick.

"I can't say I'm entirely surprised," Boomer remarked, shaking his head. "Souvlaki? What did the mamas expect?"

Jaz called Milly.

Milly was quick to arrive and retrieve the dog. "I'll take him to my shelter while I try to find his owner," she assured us, giving the Greek mamas a thumbs-up for their efforts, which earned her a frown from Nik.

Our next stop led us to a residential neighborhood on the other end of town where another trap had been triggered. As we approached, we heard a rustling sound. This time, it wasn't a dog but a mischievous raccoon nibbling on a piece of baklava.

Nik ran a hand through his disheveled thick, dark hair. "Since when do snakes like baklava? Of course, the meddling mamas are MIA. Raccoons can be mean, especially when cornered, no matter how sweet their treat."

Boomer called animal control, who arrived with a team to safely capture the raccoon and release it in a suitable area.

"Where in Hades are they?" I muttered, looking around at the growing spectators emerging from their homes. The rumor mill was going to have a field day with this one. "I have a bad feeling about this."

As the day wore on, we received yet another call about a trap going off near the town's historic library. By now, we were used to surprises, but nothing could have prepared us for what we found.

There, amidst the bushes, was a wailing Aunt Tasoula, her camo outfit now streaked with the pungent smell of skunk spray. She'd set the skunk free from the trap, but had paid the ultimate price. Ma and Chloe were holding their noses, their eyes watering fiercely as they ran away from her.

"Oh, woe is me. Why I get Pepé Le Pee-yew?" she exclaimed, waving her arms in frustration. "Ungrateful critter."

I'd never been this close to a skunk spray before. It was so much stronger than I ever realized up close. I could barely keep my eyes open, they were burning so badly. I could see why Aunt Tasoula's eyes were mere slits surrounded by runny black mascara.

Jasper and Emily were already there, Emily going live with her followers, capturing every moment of the chaos. "This is gold!" she exclaimed, her phone trained on Aunt Tasoula, who was valiantly trying to mask the smell with a piece of spanakopita.

Nik looked at me. "This one's all you, Ballas."

Boomer nodded at Jaz. "Call animal control, Babe. I'm out."

They left the scene and headed back to their own investigation.

Jaz and I, on the other hand, took Aunt Tasoula to her spa for a much-needed tomato bath.

Ma, ever the healer, offered in a nasally voice from the cotton balls stuffed up her nostrils, "Let me squirt you with Aloe. It make Pepé Perfume."

"Just let me die, Ophelia," Aunt Tasoula grumbled, sinking into the tub of tomato juice. "I no smell pretty again. Tate no like me no more."

"Tate's a smitten kitten," Chloe said with a clothespin pinching her nose tight. "Here. This baking soda paste fix you hair." She handed the mixture to Aunt Tasoula.

"It no help. I scarlet letter," she wailed. "A ... for awful aroma." But she rubbed the baking soda through her hair anyway.

"Let that sit, and we'll come check on you in a bit," I said, retreating to the waiting room with Jaz.

The smell was so bad, Aunt Tasoula cancelled all appointments and closed her shop. It would need a good cleaning before re-opening.

"What a day." Jaz laughed at the absurdity of everything that had happened.

Despite the mishaps and eccentricities, there was something endearing about the Greek mamas' determination to protect their families. That and their unwavering belief in the power of Greek food. I chuckled just thinking about it. My life was certainly never boring.

It was then that my phone rang. I answered, praying for no more bad news.

It was Nik. "Bjorn caught the two poisonous snakes," he informed me. "Apparently, he's been tracking them and setting up his own proper traps. He really does know his way around the reptiles."

"Where are they?" I asked.

"Natalie has confiscated them and is relocating them to the zoo."

Jaz looked relieved after hearing him through the phone.

"At least no one else will be at risk of dying from a snake bite," I voiced both our thoughts.

"True, but there are more kinds of snakes than just reptiles," Nik replied, adding, "We still have a killer on the loose."

"Agreed. Thanks for letting me know about the snakes, Detective."

"You got it, Ballas."

Relief washed over me as I hung up and relayed the news to the mamas.

Aunt Tasoula, still soaking in her tomato bath, gave a triumphant cheer. "See? Our plan work!"

"Your plan didn't work. Bjorn's did," I clarified.

"Ah, but only after we tell him our plan." Ma patted her chest.

"Yes, we the heroes." Chloe nodded once, not about to let her ex take credit for saving the day.

I couldn't deny it. In their own crazy way, the Greek mamas had once again proven their resourcefulness and resilience. As Jaz and I left the spa, the sun setting over the town, I felt a deep sense of gratitude for my amazing best friend and the strong, spirited women who had shaped my life.

17

I arrived home to evening shadows dancing across the driveway. As I approached the house, I could hear murmurs of conversation coming from the garage. Curious, I moved closer, recognizing the familiar voices of Nik and his father, Bjorn. They were talking, and from the tone of their voices, it felt like something serious.

I hesitated at the side entrance, my hand poised to push open the door. Instead, I lingered just outside, not wanting to interrupt. It wasn't often that Nik and Bjorn had heart-to-heart conversations, and I didn't want to disturb them. Their relationship had been rocky, primarily due to Bjorn's long absences. Ever since Bjorn had settled in Clearview, Nik had wanted to clear the air about his feelings.

"I've been meaning to talk to you about this for a while," Nik began, his voice steady but tinged with underlying emotion. "You being gone all the time ... it hurt. Ma had to do everything alone, and I had to grow up without you."

Bjorn sighed, his voice heavy with regret. "I know, drengur minn. I made a lot of mistakes. I thought I was doing the right thing by chasing opportunities, but I realize now what it cost our family."

There was a pause, and I peeked in through the window. I could see Nik's pained expression. "Now that you're back, I want to understand why. Was it really because of Ma and me? Or were you just using that as an excuse to run from your business problems in Norway?"

Bjorn hesitated before replying, "I did come here for your Ma and you. I've always loved you both, even if I wasn't good at showing it."

"But what about your business? The luxury resort," Nik pressed. "I know it went under, and I know your name was cleared of any wrongdoing, but people lost a lot of money. Someone else got arrested for it, right?"

"Yes," Bjorn admitted. "The man who got arrested was guilty of sabotage, but I don't think he was the one calling the shots. There's more to it, but I can't say anything more about that right now."

I tried to hear every word. The conversation shifted back to Chloe, a woman who had been through so much and deserved happiness.

"Nik, I never stopped loving your Ma," Bjorn confessed. "But I realized I'm not the settling down kind. I want to see her happy, truly happy. If that means letting her go, then so be it."

Nik's voice softened, "She has a chance to be happy with Captain Quincy Crenshaw. He makes her happy. If you care about her like you say you do, then you'll let her move on. We needed you a long time ago. We're okay now."

Bjorn sighed deeply. "I will. I just want to see her smile again. I love all women, but I would never hurt one. And I promise you, Nik, I did not kill Sigrid."

Nik's response was immediate as I watched him nod. "I believe you. But it would be better if you had an alibi instead of just driving around alone to think."

Bjorn hesitated for a moment like he wanted to say something before shrugging. "Sometimes a man needs to be alone with his thoughts."

The air grew tense, but then Nik shifted his attention to the workbench, where he was repairing an old rocking chair that our puppy Willow had chewed up while teething. "I'm almost done fixing this," he said, trying to lighten the mood.

"It looks good." Bjorn's voice filled with pride as watched him work and then started talking about how he had found and trapped the two poisonous snakes. "It was tricky, but I managed to secure them without anyone getting hurt."

"Yeah, how did that all happen?" Nik asked.

Bjorn continued, "I found them in an abandoned warehouse on the outskirts of town. The place was overgrown with weeds and debris, making it the perfect hiding spot for such creatures, and there's a river out back. I carefully set up traps using bait to lure them out. Patience was key; I waited for hours, making sure I didn't startle them."

I sucked in a breath, realizing he was talking about the warehouse Jaz and I went to with the secret door and tunnels. I held my breath, wondering if he found them.

"When they finally took the bait, I slowly approached with a snake stick, maintaining a safe distance. I carefully secured each snake in a cloth bag, ensuring they couldn't bite through. It was nerve-wracking but necessary to prevent any harm to the town."

Nik paused his work, listening intently to Bjorn's

tale. "That sounds terrifying. But why did you do it? Couldn't you have called Natalie?"

Bjorn shrugged, a hint of a smile playing on his lips. "Sometimes, you've got to take matters into your own hands. Besides, it was a good test of my skills and kept them sharp. Plus, I couldn't risk waiting for help when there were people in the warehouse district."

Nik nodded thoughtfully and resumed working on the rocking chair. "Still, Natalie is the expert. You could have been hurt."

"Natalie's got enough on her plate," Bjorn said in an odd voice, then cleared his throat. "So, what—"

Suddenly, Wolfgang started barking from inside the house. Nik looked toward the garage side door, and I knew my cover was blown.

Taking a deep breath, I stepped inside, trying to appear casual. "Hey, I just got home," I announced, letting the dogs into the garage with us.

Nik's gaze met mine, and I could see in his eyes that he knew I had been eavesdropping. But he let it go, a small smile tugging at the corners of his lips. "Welcome home, Kalli."

I returned his smile, grateful for his understanding.

Bjorn cleared his throat, breaking the silence. "It's good to see you, Kalli. I hope you're taking care of my boy."

I nodded, feeling a warmth spread through me. "Always, Bjorn. We take care of each other."

Nik resumed working on the rocking chair, and I joined him, handing him tools and offering support. As the evening wore on, the conversation flowed more easily. Bjorn shared stories from his time in Norway, and Nik opened up about his worries for the future. It was a night of healing, a step towards mending their fractured relationship.

When the chair was finally repaired, Nik stood back to admire his handiwork. "Looks good as new," he said, wiping his hands on a rag. "Thanks for the help, Ballas. And thanks for the talk, Dad," he added, his voice softer, more respectful.

Bjorn's eyes glistened with unshed tears. "Anytime, son. Anytime."

The three of us walked back into the house, the warmth of the home embracing us. I glanced at Nik, his expression one of contentment. Despite the turmoil we faced, there was a sense of unity, of belonging. It filled me with high hopes for the future.

As the night drew to a close, Bjorn stood to leave. "I should get going," he said, his voice tinged with reluctance.

"Thank you for coming, Dad. It means a lot to me." Nik smiled.

He smiled, a genuine warmth in his eyes. "Take care of yourself, Son. And if you ever need anything, I'm here."

With a final nod, he left, leaving behind a sense of peace. Nik and I watched him go, knowing that while their journey to reconciliation was far from over, this was a significant step in the right direction.

We spent the rest of the evening catching up. As Nik and I sat on the couch, his arm wrapped around me, I whispered, "I'm proud of you, Nik. For talking to your dad."

He kissed the top of my head, his voice tender. "Thank you, Kalli. I couldn't have done it without you."

～

THE SMELL of freshly baked goods filled the air as I stepped into *Aphrodite's* the next day.

Ma was already there, bustling around the kitchen with Aunt Tasoula. Chloe and Yiayia were at the counter, carefully measuring ingredients. My cousin Frona, with her pigtails bouncing, was washing dishes, while her sister Eleni, who had just taken a tray of cookies out of the oven, was preparing boxes. Thalia had even taken the day off from her law office to help. She was meticulously arranging the bake sale flyers.

We were all here to bake desserts for the church bake sale. *Holy Trinity Greek Orthodox Church* was still struggling. Father Papadopoulos and Sister Philothea were doing their best to entice parishioners back in, but they needed all the help they could get. So, we decided to raise money through a bake sale.

It's what Greeks do.

Ma turned to me with a smile. "Kalliope. You start on Baklava. Okay? Okay. We need many. You make more."

"Of course, Ma," I replied, tying my apron.

I glanced over at Frona, who was humming a little tune as she scrubbed the dishes. Frona was always eager to help. She loved projects of any kind. Her sister Eleni was constantly watching over her, making sure she was okay, when Yiayia was occupied.

Jasper was outside doing some repairs. He had been spending a lot of time with Emily. The match-making mamas were thrilled, but I wasn't sure if Emily liked him or if she was just fascinated by our family drama for all her followers.

Aunt Tasoula had recently cut her hair short because it still smelled like skunk from the snake trapping. Surprisingly, the new hairstyle looked chic on her. Even Tate, who she feared would be critical of her appearance, liked it better.

He would have liked her bald, he was that smitten.

As I started layering the phyllo dough for the baklava, Chloe came over to chat. "Kalli, I talk to Nik earlier today."

"Oh, really? Anything interesting?" I studied her curiously. Maybe he'd talked to his ma about our wedding?

She nodded. "I think I finally ready to let Bjorn go and say yes to Quincy's proposal for real."

"Oh," I said, dejected.

She frowned. "You no happy?"

I looked up at her, startled. "Sorry, I was lost in thought." I smiled wide, happy for her. "That's wonderful, Chloe. Quincy is a good man."

Chloe smiled, a hint of relief in her eyes. "Yes. It's time. Bjorn is my past. Quincy my future. Speaking of futures. Have you and Nik picked a wedding date yet?"

Before I could respond, everyone turned to look at me, waiting for an answer. I felt the heat rise in my cheeks and was about to stammer out an excuse when my phone rang. Jaz, my lifelong savior, was calling me just in time to save me from the interrogation.

"Sorry, I have to take this," I said, quickly stepping out of the kitchen. "Jaz, you're my lifeline," I whispered into the phone.

"Whatever I saved you from can't be worse than this."

"What's wrong?"

"You need to come to *Full Disclosure* immediately, Kalli," Jaz's voice was urgent. "Your loft has been trashed, and there's a dead snake on the lace with a note that says, 'back off or else.'"

My heart pounded in my chest. "I'll be right there."

I rushed back into the kitchen, my mind racing. "Ma, I have to go. Something's happened at my loft."

Ma's face filled with concern, but she nodded. "Go, Kalli. We manage here."

I grabbed my backpack purse and hurried out, my thoughts a jumble of fear and anger. Who would do something like this? And why?

WHEN I ARRIVED at my loft, I found the place in shambles. Furniture overturned, pictures smashed, and in the middle of the mess, a dead snake on my lace tablecloth with a menacing note. The thought of someone spreading their germs and invading my personal space had me feeling like I was going to be sick.

Jaz was waiting for me, her face a mask of worry. "I'm so sorry, Kalli. I called the police, but they haven't arrived yet."

I hugged her tightly, grateful for her support. "Thank you, Jaz. I don't know what I'd do without you."

As we waited for the police, I tried to make sense of what had happened. Did this have something to do with the bake sale? Or was it connected to something else entirely? Someone clearly didn't want me helping the church and looking into the murder investigation.

Or maybe it had to do with the underground tunnels.

The patrol officers arrived and began their investigation, but they didn't have many answers. They took my statement and promised to keep me updated. In the meantime, I felt a growing sense of unease.

This was more than just a warning—it was a threat.

Nik and Boomer were working the night shift, following their own leads. He'd heard about what happened and called me immediately, but I told him everything was okay. I didn't want to worry him any more than he already was.

So, I spent a sleepless night with the dogs curled up beside me. The next morning, I returned to *Aphrodite's*, determined to continue with the bake sale. I refused to let anything stop us from helping the church.

The kitchen was a hive of activity. Aunt Tasoula was decorating a cake, her short hair looking stylish as ever. Chloe was piping icing onto cookies, while Yiayia and Frona were making a fresh batch of dough.

"Are you okay, Kalli?" Ma asked, her eyes full of concern.

I nodded, trying to put on a brave face. "I'll be fine, Ma. We have a bake sale to prepare for."

As the day went on, we worked tirelessly, filling the boxes with delicious treats. The smell of freshly baked bread, cakes, and pastries was intoxicating. Despite the lingering fear from the previous night, there was a sense of camaraderie and purpose.

Jasper and Emily came in for a break, both looking tired but satisfied with their progress on the repairs. Emily had flour on her cheek, and Jasper couldn't stop smiling at her. I couldn't help but wonder if there was something more than just friendship between them like the mamas hoped for, but I still was worried about her true intentions.

Aunt Tasoula, ever the matchmaker, couldn't resist commenting. "Emily, you becoming Greek. You good girl. You and Jasper make good team. Maybe you spend more time together, no?"

Emily laughed, brushing the flour off her cheek. "We'll see, Aunt Tasoula. For now, I'm just happy to help, and my followers are loving watching Jasper work."

"My Jasper a gorgeous boy." Ma nodded once.

Chloe, ever perceptive, gave me a knowing look. "What about you, Kalli? Have you and Nik set a date yet?"

There was no escaping matchmaking mamas.

Before I could respond, the front door opened, and I sighed in relief. It was a delivery of supplies for the bake sale, just in time to save me from answering.

We spent the rest of the afternoon preparing for the bake sale, the atmosphere in the kitchen growing more festive with each passing hour. The shelves were filled with beautiful desserts, each one a testament to our hard work and love for the church.

Even chef Marieta made an appearance to make good on her promise of a photo of her and Ma to hang in the restaurant. Of course, she brought her security detail and a slew of photographers.

Ma was over the moon.

As the sun began to set, we took a moment to rest. Ma sat down next to me, her eyes thoughtful. "Kalli, I know you worried about what happened at you loft. But remember, you have us. You not alone."

I nodded, grateful for her words. "Thank you, Ma. I just ... I don't understand why this is happening." Ma was proud of my designer skills, but she never cared for me designing what she called naughty clothes. She had, however, come to respect my decision to do so.

She patted my hand, a reassuring smile on her face. "Sometimes, the world is strange place. But as long as we have each other, we face anything." *And then you come work with me some day.*

"Maybe," I said.

She puckered her forehead. "Maybe what?"

I sometimes forgot that only Jaz and Nik knew I could read minds. "Maybe we should set up. The bake sale's about to start. But thanks, Ma. You're the best."

"I know." Her cheeks flushed candy apple red, and she cupped my cheek with her palm. "You right. Let's go."

THE BAKE SALE was a huge success.

People from all over the community came to support us, buying our delicious treats and donating generously. Father Papadopoulos and Sister Philothea were overjoyed, their faces beaming with gratitude.

As the night drew to a close, I felt a sense of accomplishment and relief. Despite the threat hanging over me, we had come together as a family and a community to support our church.

Jasper and Emily stayed to help clean up, their laughter filling the air. I couldn't help but smile at the sight of them working side by side. Maybe Ma and Aunt Tasoula were right—maybe there was something more between them, and I was worrying for nothing.

As we finished cleaning up, I glanced around at my family, my heart swelling with love and gratitude.

Nik called me. "Kalli, how are you? I know you said you were fine, but I also know *you*. Be honest with me, Ballas."

I took a deep breath, trying to steady my voice. "I'm fine now, Nik, I promise. It's been a rough couple of days, but we got through the bake sale, and it was a huge success."

"I'm so proud of you," he said, his voice filled with warmth. "I wish I could have been there with you."

"It's okay. I just want this case over with already," I replied, my heart aching with longing.

"Me too. I'm gonna work the nightshift again and see what I can find out."

"Okay. Stay safe."

THE NEXT MORNING, I woke up to find a message from the police. They had a lead on who might be behind the attack on my loft. It wasn't much, but it was a start. I squared my shoulders. We would find out who was behind this, and we would stop them for good this time.

18

The morning sun cast a golden glow over the church as I made my way up the stone steps. The scent of freshly baked pastries still clung to my clothes from yesterday's bake sale. I inhaled deeply, savoring the lingering aroma of warm bread and organic honey-dipped pastries. The garden surrounding the church was alive with color—deep red roses, sprigs of lavender, and wild daisies that had pushed their way through the cracks in the old stone wall.

Despite everything happening in town, this place still felt peaceful.

Father Papadopoulos met me at the door, his eyes twinkling behind his wire-rimmed glasses as I handed over the envelope filled with donations. The crinkling paper was a quiet but satisfying sound, the product of everyone's hard work and generosity.

"Thank you, Kalli," he said warmly, his voice like a summer breeze. "This will help us tremendously."

Sister Philothea clasped her hands together, beaming as if the sun had broken through the clouds. "The community has been so generous. We are truly blessed."

I smiled, feeling a warmth spread through my chest. "I'm just glad we could help. It was a team effort." The words felt sweet on my tongue, a moment of goodness amid the dark cloud that had taken over our little town.

"See you in church, young lady." Father grinned.

I saluted him on my way out. But as I stepped outside, that brief sense of peace was shattered.

Bjorn was still in the church garden, working on the ongoing snake infestation problem. Every time he and Natalie made progress, more snakes appeared. It was almost as if someone was bringing more in. His shirt clung to him with sweat, his muscles flexing as he worked with focused determination so like his son. The sun caught the blond strands in his hair, giving him an almost ethereal glow, but my attention was drawn to the tension in his body.

Something was wrong.

Just as I was about to call out to him, a woman approached from the opposite side of the garden. Ingrid was still in town? I hadn't seen her in a while. Her usual composed expression was tight with urgency, her jaw set in a firm line. The sight of her filled me with a sense of unease.

Sensing something serious was going on, I ducked behind a lush cluster of rose bushes close to them, their petals brushing against my skin as I crouched low, listening intently.

Bjorn wiped his hands on a cloth and turned to her, arching a thick blond eyebrow. "Ingrid, what are you doing here?"

She set her jaw, glancing around before speaking. "We need to talk."

"This isn't the time or place. Besides, we've said all there is to say."

Her lips pressed into a thin line. "That resort would have revolutionized tourism with eco-friendly innovations."

Bjorn's eyes darkened, his expression turning unreadable. "I can make it up to you. We can build another resort someplace else. One that doesn't involve land tied up in legal disputes."

"No one is going to want to invest in anything we do after our last investors' funds vanished into offshore accounts." She leveled him with a glare. "And I'm not sure I can trust you again."

"I told you I didn't know about it." His jaw hardened. "And I'm not going to stop looking until I find out who hired the mole. I'll get that money back if it's the last thing I do."

Before she could say anything else, Natalie came running up, her face flushed and her breath coming in quick gasps. "Niles and Theo are snooping around the landscaping again with a metal detector," she explained, her eyes flashing with anger like storm clouds brewing on the horizon. "What do they need a metal detector for? They're going to ruin all the progress we've made on the grounds."

I held my breath. They had to be looking for the snake key Nik found.

Bjorn's grip tightened on the cloth in his hands. I could see the muscles in his arms tense as he followed her gaze toward Niles Turner and Theo Harris.

Bjorn stormed over to them, with Ingrid and Natalie close behind.

I darted over behind a tree closer to them to keep listening.

"What do you think you're doing, Turner?" Bjorn ground out, his voice low and dangerous.

Niles turned slowly, a smirk playing at the corners

of his lips. "What's it to you, Stevens?" His voice dripped with contempt.

"This isn't your property. You can't just go around doing whatever you want to it," Bjorn ground out.

"Why not? Sigrid wasn't yours, either, yet that didn't stop you," Niles spat back. "And now she's dead."

"You can't blame that on Bjorn," Natalie interjected.

"I can and *did* do whatever I wanted to Bjorn, and he deserved it!" Niles shouted, losing his cool for a moment.

A moment was all it took

Ingrid's eyes widened then filled with rage. "You're the mastermind behind the mole!"

Bjorn snapped. "You ruined everything!" he shouted, lunging at Niles.

The two men grappled, fists flying in a fit of rage, their grunts and curses filling the air. Bjorn was a much bigger man, but Niles was fast and mean.

My heart pounded as I fumbled for my phone, fingers trembling as I sent a text to Nik.

Get here now. It's about to explode.

As I pressed send, Niles broke free and reached into his jacket.

A gun.

The silver glint of the weapon caught the sunlight, and I felt my stomach drop. No matter how strong Bjorn was, muscles were no match for a gun.

Theo, usually cocky and self-assured, took a step back, his face paling. "Whoa, Niles, calm down, man. Put the gun away. This isn't going to solve anything," he said, his voice surprisingly shaky for a man who prided himself on being unflinching.

Niles' eyes blazed with a madness I had never seen

before. "Stay out of this, Theo," he growled, waving the gun threateningly in Bjorn's direction. "This is between me and him."

Bjorn didn't back down, his fists still clenched. "You think a gun is going to fix what you did? You destroyed everything I worked for, and for what? Because Sigrid chose me? You're pathetic."

Niles let out a bitter laugh, the sound cold and hollow. "That's exactly why, Bjorn. I planted the mole in your company to take the fall. I wanted to ruin your business, make you lose everything, so Sigrid would see you for the failure you are. But even when she followed you to Clearview, even when you had nothing, she still wanted you." His face took on a crazed expression. "That's when I knew it was over."

Theo looked sick. "You really did all of this over her? Did you—"

Niles' grip on the gun tightened, his knuckles turning white. "She was mine," he hissed, cutting him off.

"Sigrid's gone. You need to let this go," Theo pleaded.

As I listened, every word felt like a dagger, cutting deeper into the twisted truth. The air was thick with tension, the weight of Niles' confession settling over us like a dark cloud. I knew I had to do something, but what could I do against a man with a gun?

I glanced down at my phone, my fingers trembling as I typed another frantic message.

He has a gun. Hurry.

I hit send, praying that help would arrive before it was too late.

Niles' eyes flicked to the side for just a second. My heart stopped. Had he seen me? I pressed myself against the tree, trying to make myself as small and inconspicuous as possible.

Bjorn's voice cut through the silence, low and furious. "You're pathetic, Niles. Sigrid was a person, not a possession."

Niles raised the gun, pointing it directly at Bjorn's chest. "Shut up!" he shouted, his voice breaking. "You don't get to talk about her. Not after what you did."

I held my breath, my mind racing. The situation was spiraling out of control, and I was helpless to stop it. All I could do was stay hidden and hope that Nik would arrive in time to prevent a tragedy.

I waited for Niles to look away for a moment and then darted behind a stack of wooden crates near the back of the church, my heart pounding so hard I feared Niles might hear it. The musty scent of damp wood and aged stone filled my nose, mixing with the faint, acrid smell of sweat and something more pungent—snake musk. Like the kind I had smelled in the warehouse. Was that how the snakes were brought into town? Were these boxes how the snakes got on church ground?

I forced myself to breathe slowly, evenly, keeping my body still as I listened.

"Pathetic? More like brilliant." Niles's voice was low but full of smug satisfaction. "Theo made me an offer too good to pass up. Sabotage the church where your family goes. All I had to do was make sure the Greeks believed the snakes were bad luck, not good, so the church would suffer financially, and the diocese would sell. Theo will cut me in on the profits from the condos. Seemed easy enough." He let out a dry chuckle. "Didn't count on the Greeks being so stubborn."

Theo's response was tight with frustration. "You

assured me they would leave, especially after planting the snakes on church grounds and in their businesses. You're not getting anything."

Niles scoffed. "I underestimated their loyalty to the church and to the stupid legend. They stuck around even with the slimy creatures in their basements and gardens. But hey, I did my part. It's not my fault they didn't scare so easy. You owe me."

From my position, I could see the tension in Theo's posture, his hands clenching and unclenching at his sides. His normally smooth demeanor was cracking, frustration leaking through.

Before Theo could respond, heavy footsteps interrupted them.

Nik.

"Niles Turner! Drop the weapon!" Nik's voice sliced through the air, sharp and authoritative. "I've heard all I need to."

Niles barely had time to react before Nik was on him, grabbing the gun from his hand and twisting his arm behind his back. Niles let out a strangled cry of pain, struggling against Nik's grip, but it was no use.

"Where the hell did you come from?" Niles growled.

I emerged from my hiding spot, waving my phone in his direction.

Bjorn, Ingrid, and Natalie gasped.

Niles and Theo gave me looks to kill.

"You're under arrest for fraud and embezzlement," Nik continued, his tone as cold as a northeast wind. He turned his glare to Theo. "And you, for obstruction of justice."

Theo made a move to run, but Boomer, appearing from around the corner, was on him in seconds, cuffing his hands. "You heard the man. You're not going anywhere."

Theo scoffed. "Obstruction? That's a stretch."

"Last I checked, releasing the abominable creatures all over town to distract us from our investigation is pretty obstructive." Boomer grunted, his face twisted in disgust. "For that alone, I'm going to enjoy you rotting in jail."

Nik smirked. "I haven't even gotten to the good part." He pulled a folded paper from his pocket. "Did you ever bother to read the church deed?"

Theo frowned. "What are you talking about?"

Nik's eyes gleamed. "If the church fails and condos go up, the land reverts to a Blackheart descendant. Not you."

Theo's face drained of color. "You're lying."

Nik shrugged. "Go ahead and check for yourself. Thalia has proof. What can I say? It pays to have a lawyer in the family. Looks like all your scheming was for nothing. The diocese wouldn't be able to sell even if they wanted to."

Theo's mouth twisted in rage. "You son of a—"

Boomer towered over him. "Easy there, snake boy. I'll take it from here, Nik," he rumbled, grabbing Theo and Niles, jerking them towards his patrol car as he read them their Miranda rights.

As Boomer guided them into the police vehicle, another voice cut through the tension.

"Where is she?" an angry male voice growled.

I stiffened as a man in a business suit stormed in, his face flushed. His eyes locked onto Natalie, and he shook his head, looking disappointed. Then he turned a gaze filled with hatred on Bjorn, who stood rigid near the landscaping.

"You slept with my wife?" His voice was low, shaking with barely restrained fury.

Bjorn didn't move; his face unreadable. "It was one night."

"She was lonely," the man spat, "because I travel for work. And you took advantage of that?"

Bjorn exhaled, his jaw tightening. "It was a mistake. I own that."

Natalie stepped forward, her face pale. "I'm so sorry, Erik. I love you."

Her husband let out a bitter laugh. "Love me? You expect me to believe that after what I just read?" He held up her phone, the screen lit with text messages.

I held my breath. This was a disaster.

Bjorn's voice was calm and steady. "I didn't mean to hurt anyone. I put my own future in jeopardy by not calling on her as my alibi just to protect her from a scandal, and now you're calling her out. Think about what you're throwing away."

Natalie's husband's hands clenched into fists, his body shaking with barely controlled anger. But instead of throwing a punch, he exhaled sharply and turned to his wife. "We're talking. Now."

She nodded quickly, following him to his car in the parking lot.

"I hate to say it, but for once, your wayward ways worked to your advantage because now you have an alibi," Nik said, shaking his head.

Bjorn nodded slowly as he stood there for a long moment, staring after them. The weight of it all seemed to settle on his shoulders.

I let out a slow, careful breath.

Bjorn was cleared.

The real criminals were caught.

It was finally over.

19

"I 'm so glad it's over," I said to Jaz a couple days later while we were at work in *Full Disclosure*.

"Nik has to be relieved," she said. "Do you think Bjorn will stick around?"

I shrugged. "I don't know. He's the restless sort, and he did agree to let Chloe go so she can finally move on with her life. Speaking of moving on with your life, where are you and Boomer going on your honeymoon?"

"I'm not sure. Once they have everything wrapped up here, he said he has a surprise for me."

"Well, that's exciting." I smiled, then my smile slipped. "I'm hoping maybe now Nik will be open to setting a wedding date, but he hasn't even brought it up."

"I'm sure he will. You know, once the dust settles."

"Speaking of dust, I'd better get to work." I headed up to my loft to work on a few Kalli Original lingerie commissions.

I had gone full rubber gloves and mask to thoroughly clean and sanitize everything in my loft myself. I didn't trust anyone else to do the job to my satisfaction. Thank Zeus I had already finished Jaz's lingerie before the horrible offense.

I took a deep breath and got to work.

A short time later the familiar chime of the bell above the door downstairs signaled someone entering the boutique. I was in the middle of adjusting a delicate lace display when I turned to see Samuel Brooks standing at the top of the stairs with sanitized hands.

"May I enter?" He arched a brow.

I nodded.

He carried himself with that investigative journalist air—sharp eyes that missed nothing, a notepad tucked into his jacket pocket, and a presence that suggested he was always two steps ahead of everyone else.

"Samuel," I greeted, dusting off my hands. "It's good to see you out of the hospital. To what do I owe the pleasure of your visit?"

The scent of vanilla and sandalwood from my candles mingled with the faint musk of late summer air that clung to his clothes. He glanced around, taking in the soft glow of my safe space's ambient lighting, the rich reds and blush pinks of satin and lace, the faint melody of jazz humming through the speakers.

"I see you redecorated after the break-in," he said with an approving nod before his gaze settled on me.

"I needed a change so I wouldn't be reminded."

"Did they ever catch the culprit?"

I shook my head. "The cameras only caught a shadowed figure dressed in black."

"Clearly, it's the same person from the church grounds and fair. Someone with a vested interest in snakes who thinks you're getting a bit too close to the truth."

I nodded. "That was Nik's thinking as well. I don't know if we'll ever find the person. I'm just glad the investigation into Sigrid's death is over and so are the snake infestations. The church and Clearview itself are finally safe."

"I don't know as I believe that *everything* has been wrapped up, maybe just Bjorn and Ingrid's situation."

I folded my arms, tilting my head. "You've changed your tune?"

His lips quirked in something that wasn't quite a smile. "I'll admit, I had my doubts. But I'm satisfied now—Bjorn and Ingrid weren't involved in the downfall of their business. The mole was placed to sabotage them, and they were just the collateral damage."

I let out a slow breath, some of the tension in my shoulders easing. "That's good to hear. But I get the feeling that's not the only reason you're here."

"You'd be right." He stepped closer, the wooden floor creaking slightly under his weight, then he sat on a chair.

"I still think Niles and Theo are mixed up in something more than just their greedy attempt to force the church under. The snake key, the rumors about an underground ring operating around the church—it's all too connected to ignore."

I studied him for a beat, his dark eyes unreadable but expectant. I decided to confide in him and see what he knew. "Niles admitted something to Nik after his arrest." I leaned against the edge of my counter, the smooth marble cool beneath my fingertips.

"Interesting. I'm listening."

"Niles told Nik he overheard Evangeline talking about the snake keys with Oliver from his research on the church, which is what made Niles start searching for them. That's why he was poking around *Rockwell Jewelers*, why he had Theo snooping around the grounds with metal detectors, and why he even checked the pond with the eels. He was looking for money—another scam, another opportunity."

Samuel's brow furrowed, and he scratched the stubble on his jaw. "So, according to Niles, he wasn't part of anything beyond the fake snake infestation scheme?"

I nodded. "That's what he claims. Just wanted to drive the Greeks out, so the church would go under, and Theo could get his hands on the land. He swears he didn't know about anything deeper. Then again, he also swears he didn't kill Sigrid, so who knows what the truth actually is."

Samuel's gaze flicked to the window, as if considering the weight of my words. Outside, rain fell lazily against the darkening sky, coating the sidewalks in a misty shower. When he looked back at me, something flickered in his expression—something sharper.

"I've been doing my own snooping," he admitted, his voice dropping a notch. "And I think Evangeline has one of the keys."

A chill that had nothing to do with the air conditioner crept over my skin. "Evangeline?" I suddenly wondered if maybe she could be the person dressed in black.

"She's too invested in the legend of the snakes and the history of the church," he said, leaning against the counter beside me. "I know she's a historian and all about preservation, but I'm thinking she's desperate. Too much of what's happened ties back to her. She knew about the snake keys long before Niles ever did. She's been acting like just another gossipy local, but I think she knows more than she lets on."

I exhaled slowly, my breath stirring the wisp of hair that had fallen loose from my updo. "And if she has one of the keys?"

"Then we need to find out why," Samuel said simply. "And what she's hiding."

The air between us was thick with unspoken questions, the kind that made my pulse quicken and my mind race with possibilities. And just like that, my peace was gone. The key wasn't just a symbol—it was a piece of a puzzle that was still missing too many parts, and there was more than one of them.

Samuel straightened. "I don't think this thing with the church is over, Kalli. Not by a long shot."

I swallowed hard, gripping the counter just a little tighter. "No," I murmured. "I don't think so either."

~

ON MY LUNCH BREAK, I headed to the historical society to talk to Evangeline.

As I entered the historical society office, the musty scent of old books and parchment greeted me. Evangeline looked up from her desk, her eyes narrowing slightly when she saw me. I wasted no time, crossing the room with determined strides.

"Evangeline," I began, my voice steady, "I brought you some of Ma's baklava. I want to thank you for being so vigilant on trying to preserve the legend of the snakes and looking out so that nothing taints the history of our beloved Greek orthodox church."

"Well, it's my job after all." She nodded once, her hair looking a far sight better than her Medusa-do.

"And you're so good at it." I set the dessert on her desk.

She relaxed a little and puffed out her chest. "I take great pride in our heritage. Mustn't let anything come in the way of that"

"Well, I for one, am glad Sigrid's murder has been solved, and that Niles has been arrested."

"Yes, I am quite thankful that the snake infestations are over." She smoothed her hair back into place.

"Can you believe Theo was behind that? I'm so glad he was arrested for obstructing justice. Now the church will be safe from being taken for a condo development."

She nodded, a tight smile on her lips. "Yes, it's all been quite a relief, but we can't let our guard down, Kalli." Her gaze locked onto mine. "Nothing is truly safe. We have to remain vigilant and do whatever it takes to protect the church."

"I agree."

I reached out and squeezed her hand. *Even lying about the eels being connected to the legend and chef Marieta taking them from the church pond for her Hades' Kitchen Cookoff wasn't enough to keep those nosy tourists away. My mission isn't done yet. The church serves a purpose far greater than just the Greek religion.*

She pulled her hand away, folding them in her lap as she inhaled a shaky breath.

"You mentioned protecting the church," I echoed, my gaze piercing hers. "From what, exactly?" And what other purpose could the church serve?

Evangeline's eyes flickered with a mix of determination and something darker. "From anyone who dares to disrupt its sanctity. You know as well as I do that there are forces at play here that won't stop until they've taken everything from us. I refuse to allow that to happen. I will go forth and prosper like a good parishioner."

Her conviction was unsettling, but I couldn't shake the feeling that she was hiding more than she let on. "You're so knowledgeable. Do you know anything about the snake key Nik found on the grounds?" I pressed, looking for a reaction. "I hear there are more than one."

Her face looked guilty, but she said, "I don't know what you're talking about."

"Oh, because Niles mentioned he heard about the key from you. That's why he's been snooping around, looking for more. Maybe he overheard you and the professor talking. Or maybe Father? Do the keys have something to do with the church history?"

She hesitated, her body stiffening slightly. "Oh, those keys. The keys are part of the church's legacy— its protection. But they're also a symbol of power, and there are those who would use them for their own gain."

"How so?"

"The less you know the better, my dear. For your protection."

"Are you one of the key holders?" I asked.

Silence filled the space between us.

"Goodness, no, my dear. Those keys are ancient. They're locked up in some vault, if around at all."

"Then how did Nik find one on the grounds?"

"It was probably buried decades ago, but with the grounds being torn up with landscaping projects and all the snakes pushing their way to the surface, it must have been unearthed accidentally."

"Where are the other two?"

"I have no idea. I really must get back to work now. Thank you for stopping by and thank your ma for the dessert."

The air between us crackled with unspoken tension. I had to find out what she was planning and how far she was willing to go to protect the church.

"Of course." I shut the door behind me. As I

walked out of the historical society office, my mind raced with the possibilities. Evangeline's desperation was clear, and I couldn't shake the feeling that Samuel was right.

Evangeline Marinakis was somehow involved.

THE HUMID AIR clung to my skin as I paced the cracked pavement outside Nik's office, the scent of damp earth and late-summer wildflowers thick in the night. The stars flickered above Clearview like scattered diamonds, their glow dimmed by the warm haze rolling in from the coast.

I was restless. I had been since Evangeline's story about eels first began to unravel.

When Nik finally stepped outside, rubbing his temple, I wasted no time.

"She lied," I said, my voice low but firm.

Nik sighed, his blue eyes sharp in the dim light. "Which part?"

"All of it." I crossed my arms. "Evangeline never saw anyone stealing those eels. There was no grand poaching operation. And they aren't even connected to the legend. She just needed a distraction—needed to keep people's eyes on something else while she worked."

Nik didn't look surprised. If anything, he looked like he had been expecting it. "Then I guess it's a good thing I've got my own news," he said. "Dale isn't just some harmless groundskeeper. He's an ex-con."

My stomach twisted. "What?"

"Smuggling," Nik said, watching my reaction carefully. "He ran with a crew out of Boston years ago. Got caught moving stolen goods through underground networks. Jewelry, antiques ... valuables people wanted to disappear."

The weight of his words settled on me. "Like an ancient key," I murmured.

Nik nodded. "I got a tip that Dale found one of them. And he's planning to sell it. Tonight."

A chill crept down my spine, despite the warmth of the evening. "To whom?"

Nik's jaw tightened. "That's what we're going to find out."

We made our way to the tunnels beneath the library. I guided him past the one to the woods and down the one that led to the church. The tunnels beneath the church were suffocating. The scent of damp stone and decay filled my nose, mixing with the faint tang of mildew and something more metallic—rust or blood, I couldn't be sure.

Nik led the way, flashlight low, his gun holstered but ready. I followed close behind, my own pulse a steady drumbeat in my ears.

We heard them before we saw them. Footsteps echoed off the tunnel walls, slow and deliberate. Then, a voice—Dale's.

"You're late."

Another voice, smooth and confident. "Patience, Dale. You have no idea how difficult it is to move around unnoticed in a town like this."

Evangeline.

I sucked in a breath, pressing myself against the cold stone wall. Nik's hand brushed against mine in a silent warning. *Wait.*

I nodded my understanding.

A flicker of light bounced off the rough tunnel walls as Dale lifted something into view—a small, tarnished key with an intricate snake design coiled around the bow.

Evangeline reached for it, her excitement—more like obsession—palpable. "I assume you want payment in cash?"

Nik moved fast.

In a blink, he lunged, tackling Dale to the ground. The key skittered across the dirt as Dale let out a strangled curse. I didn't have time to process it before Evangeline scrambled to pick it up and then turned to run.

"Oh, no, you don't." I grabbed her wrist, twisting her arm behind her back as she fought against me, heels scraping against the stone floor.

"Get off me!" she shrieked. *You don't know what you're doing. I'm the chosen one to protect the church's legacy.*

"You're not chosen, you're a liar. You lied about the eels," I said, my grip tightening on her arm. "You made up that whole story, didn't you?"

Evangeline stilled, gasping. "How did you—"

"That's why you bought the snakes, too," I pressed. "You wanted to scare her off. But when that didn't work, you started making up stories to keep us all chasing our tails."

Nik wrenched Dale's arms behind his back, snapping handcuffs into place. "You're done, Dale. We know your history. We know what you've been doing down here."

Dale just glared, lips pressed into a tight, defiant line. "You have no idea what you've done."

Evangeline huffed, shaking her head. "You're grasping at straws."

"Am I?" Nik took the key from her pocket, turning

it over in his fingers. "Then why were you about to buy this?"

Evangeline said nothing.

Dale scowled. "You don't know a damn thing."

Nik sighed, talking while hauling him back toward the tunnel entrance. "You're under arrest for theft, smuggling, conspiracy, and anything else I can think of."

I followed closely behind with a quiet Evangeline. Even her thoughts were silent for once.

Boomer's voice echoed from the tunnel entrance. "Took you long enough."

We hauled them out of the tunnels, where Samuel was waiting with a triumphant grin. "Finally," he said, scribbling furiously in his notepad. "This will make one hell of a story."

As the authorities took Dale and Evangeline away, I felt a strange mix of relief and exhaustion. We had done it. The mystery was solved. Marieta would be cleared of the eel theft and be free to go.

Nik and I stood together, watching as the last of the summer sun dipped below the horizon. "I couldn't have done this without you, Ballas," he said softly.

"Good to hear you're finally recognizing my talents, Detective." I slipped my arm around him.

He chuckled, pulling me in tight. "Oh, I appreciate all of your talents." *And I plan to show you just how much when we get home.*

Home.

Nothing sounded better at the moment, and hopefully now everything could get back on track.

20

The scent of incense drifted through the Greek Orthodox Church, mingling with the warm summer air that filtered through the open doors. Sunlight streamed in, painting the stone walls in gold and amber hues, as the familiar cadence of Father Papadopoulos' voice carried through the nave.

"Let us give thanks," he said, his voice rich with emotion, "for the truth has been revealed, and our house of worship is no longer shadowed by deceit."

Sister Philothea stood beside him, hands clasped, her face a mask of serene gratitude.

The pews were full again, the parishioners no longer afraid of the rumors that had kept them away. The scandal of the murder, and the snake-infested grounds had nearly destroyed this place, but now, the congregation had returned.

I sat near the front with my Ma, Aunt Tasoula, and Chloe. Next to us was Chef Marieta, her usual air of confidence tinged with relief.

She smoothed the skirt of her floral dress, looking unusually sentimental. "At last, my name is cleared, and I can move on with my life."

"You were falsely accused, Marieta," I said. "It's only right that your reputation be restored."

She smiled. "And now, I can continue my tour without baggage."

Nik leaned in from the row behind me, his breath warm against my ear. "We should set a date soon," he murmured.

I tensed, feeling the weight of three sets of expectant mama eyes on me. "Uh-huh," I muttered, secretly relieved, yet surprised he'd say so in front of the mamas.

"Don't 'uh-huh' me," Ma said, swatting my arm. "We past the uh-huh stage."

Chloe chimed in, "You two need to make it official. Make nice Greek babies."

Nik chuckled. "Ma, I'm only half Greek and Kalli is adopted. How Greek can our babies be?"

The mamas all gasped and made the sign of the cross.

Aunt Tasoula huffed. "Enough! We sit down tonight and plan this properly."

I barely had time to protest before Marieta stood, smoothing her dress again. "Well, I'll miss this town. Truly."

I turned to look at her. "Your flight isn't until tomorrow morning."

"True," she said, glancing at the door. "But why waste time lingering when there's so much more to see?"

In Clearview? A strange sensation prickled at the back of my mind. I reached out my hand to shake hers. "It's been lovely getting to know someone of your talents."

"Thank you." *My talent lies in my secret ingredients, and I don't plan to leave until I get what I paid for. Even if*

I have to get it myself.

I stiffened, my gaze snapping to hers as she let go of my hand and started to walk away.

I stood abruptly. "I think I'll walk you out."

She laughed lightly. "That's not necessary."

"Sure it is," I said, my voice sharper than I intended. "Greek hospitality."

Nik gave me a puzzled look.

I smiled overly bright, hoping he would catch on that I'd heard her thoughts and something was up. Then I hurried after Marieta while he headed over to pay his respects to Father and Sister.

As we stepped outside, the mamas followed without question, not wanting to miss any action. But Marieta was fast. The moment we hit the courtyard, she veered to the side, claiming she forgot something, and vanished into another part of the church.

"That rude," Aunt Tasoula said. "Maybe I still smell like skunk."

Ma crossed her arms. "She disappear like ghost."

Chloe exhaled. "She know something we don't. Let's bust her."

"Who else you gonna call." Ma shrugged.

"Father's still greeting parishioners," I noted. "She's hiding somewhere in there."

Nik caught up to us. "What's going on?"

I explained in quick, hushed words. He nodded. "We'll need someone who knows the layout of this place better than we do."

A voice interrupted us. "I might be able to help."

We turned to see Cole, the church's maintenance man. He scratched the back of his head, his expression hesitant.

"I found a hidden chamber a few days ago," he admitted. "Haven't told Father yet—thought it might be nothing, but if she's trying to hide..."

"Show us," Nik ordered.

Cole led us to a narrow passage behind the altar, pushing aside an old wooden panel. A faint musty smell drifted out.

"Wait here," Nik told the mamas, then motioned for me to follow.

The mamas ignored him, of course.

The tunnel was damp, the stone walls pressing in around us. Cole led us deeper until we reached a heavy iron door secured with a rusted lock that I was betting a snake key would open. Nik took the bolt cutters from Cole, snapping the lock with one decisive motion. The door creaked open, revealing a dimly lit chamber.

And there she was.

Marieta sat bound to a chair, gagged, her eyes wild with fury.

"What the—" I gasped, running to untie her. "Who did this?"

Cole backed away, hands raised. "I swear, I had nothing to do with this!"

Nik grabbed his shirt. "Then who did?"

Marieta coughed once the gag was removed. "You think he did this?" she hissed. "He saved me! She is the one who tied me up!"

A shadow moved at the entrance.

Sister Philothea.

The soft, kind face I had known twisted into something sharper, colder. Something non nun-like. She held a gun, the muzzle trained on us. "You just couldn't leave well enough alone, could you?"

Nik pulled me behind him, his muscles tensing. "Who are you really?"

She smiled a sinister smile and peeled off her habit. "My real name is Phylis Blackheart. And I am the rightful heir to this land."

Marieta groaned. "Oh, not this nonsense again."

Phylis' grip on the gun tightened. "You think this is a joke? My family has been running this operation for generations under the guise of the church. The tunnels, the smuggling—it's all ours."

Nik's jaw clenched. He took a careful step forward, his hands loose at his sides, but I knew that tension in his body—he was ready to move. "So, you've been using the church as a cover for smuggling this whole time," he said. "What exactly are you bringing in?"

Phylis smirked. "Exotic animals. Ivory. Rare artifacts. Whatever my buyers want." Her gaze flicked to Marieta. "She's one of my best customers."

Marieta scowled. "I didn't pay for this kind of service."

I looked at her, horrified. "You knew?"

She sighed, rolling her shoulders now that she was free. "I bought what I needed, Kalli. Do you know how hard it is to source rare meats for an exclusive restaurant?"

"What about Greek loyalty and tradition?" I demanded.

Marieta gave me a slow, disdainful once-over. "What do you care? You're not really Greek."

The words punched me in the gut. But before I could respond, Ma was suddenly there, moving faster than I'd ever seen her.

Crack.

Her hand collided with Marieta's cheek in a perfect slap, the sound echoing off the stone walls. "Get out of my sight," Ma hissed.

"You no Greek," Aunt Tasoula spat.

"You imposter," Chloe sneered.

Marieta stumbled, clutching her face, looking genuinely stunned. But Phylis wasn't finished.

"Enough," she snapped, raising the gun again. "None of you are leaving here."

A movement behind her made my breath catch— Nik saw it, too, and I knew what was coming before it happened.

Phylis sensed it a second too late.

Boom.

The impact knocked the gun from her hand as Boomer barreled into her. She crashed against the stone wall, stunned, and Oliver rushed in. Nik lunged, pinning her arms before she could recover.

"Give it up," Oliver said, stepping forward, gun drawn. He looked at Phylis with something close to disappointment. "You almost got away with it."

Phylis thrashed against Nik's grip, but it was useless. "How?" she spat. "How did you know?"

Oliver sighed. "Dale was my informant. He's been helping me track this operation for years. And Father has been a big help with the church's history."

I blinked. "Wait—you're not a retired Anthropology professor?"

Nik huffed a humorless laugh. "I'm guessing not."

Oliver shrugged. "Undercover FBI. And Dale, well —he used to be in the game. But he wanted out."

Phylis sneered. "He was weak."

Oliver's gaze hardened. "He was trying to make amends."

Oliver moved in, securing Phylis with zip ties. She didn't resist this time. Maybe she knew it was over.

I turned to Marieta. "And what about her?"

Oliver studied her for a long moment. "She's under arrest, too."

Marieta lifted her chin. "For what? Buying legally imported ingredients?"

Oliver smirked. "You and I both know your purchases weren't legal. Not to mention, cooking exotic animals that are often endangered is just wrong."

"Tell that to my lawyers." Marieta exhaled sharply, like she was annoyed more than anything. "Well. This is inconvenient."

I rolled my eyes, disgusted with her. "You think?"

As the agents led them away, I let out a breath I hadn't realized I was holding. It was over for real this time.

Nik turned to me, his expression softening. "Are you okay?"

I nodded. "Just ... processing."

Ma stepped up, gripping my hand. "Come, we need support Father Papadopoulos like he do us. And we can talk about when he free to marry you."

And just like that ... we were back.

EPILOGUE

We were finally home, settled in with our pets—Wolfgang, Willow, and Prissy. The house was a cacophony of warm, familiar sounds, and for the first time in what felt like ages, Willow was sleeping through the night.

I glanced over at Nik, who was leaning against the kitchen counter, a gentle smile playing on his lips.

"What has you in such a good mood?" It had been a while since he'd looked so relaxed and at peace.

"Ma finally accepted Captain Quincy Crenshaw's wedding proposal," he said, his eyes reflecting genuine happiness. "For real this time."

"That's wonderful!" I exclaimed, feeling the warmth spread through my chest. "And Bjorn and Ingrid? How are they?"

"Off to Sweden to start a new business venture," Nik replied, his voice filled with pride. "They're excited."

"Let's hope this one pans out." I laughed.

"No kidding. We do much better long distance." His gaze softened. "But it was nice seeing him and clearing the air about things we should have settled years ago."

"I'm so happy for you, and that I finally got to meet the Viking." I laughed.

"He certainly lives up to his name."

"You have his size, but your hair and facial features ... That's all your mama." I winked.

"Thank the gods," he agreed.

"And Natalie?" I asked, curious about our herpetologist's latest news.

"She and her husband are going to couples counseling. They're determined to work things out," Nik said.

"Good for them." I took a deep breath, feeling the weight of recent events slowly lifting. "Emily is sticking around to give dating Jasper a real try," I shared. "Her followers are all for it and want to see more of them together."

Nik laughed softly. "That's great, if the mamas don't scare her away first. And Boomer? How did Jaz react to the honeymoon surprise?"

"Oh, Jaz was over the moon!" I said, my smile widening. "I can't believe Boomer surprised her with a honeymoon in Rovinj, Croatia. It looks like such a beautiful Venetian-style coastal town with cobblestone streets, waterfront seafood restaurants, and stunning Adriatic views."

Nik's face lit up with a sparkle I hadn't seen in far too long. "Speaking of honeymoons, let's set a wedding date ourselves without anyone else's interference." None of the mamas had been able to agree on what date worked best, so we'd tabled that task.

Until now, apparently.

I hesitated, not wanting to rush anything. "We don't have to if it's too much pressure." I bit my bottom lip.

His gaze softened as he took my hand. "There's nothing I want more."

In that moment, surrounded by the love of our pets and the peacefulness of our home, I knew he meant every word.

BOOKS BY KARI LEE TOWNSEND

KALLI BALLAS MYSTERY

Mind Over Murder

Two Cents of Doom

A Touch of Malice

An Inkling of Evil

Mayhem on the Mind

Trouble for Your Thoughts

CECE MONROE MYSTERY

Harmful Habits

SUNNY MEADOWS MYSTERY

Tempest in the Tea Leaves

Corpse in the Crystal Ball

Trouble in the Tarot

Shenanigans in the Shadows

Perish in the Palm

Hazard in the Horoscope

Chaos and Cold Feet

Murder in the Meditation

Cruising into Danger

Road Trip to Ruin

DIGITAL DIVA

Talk to the Hand

Rise of the Phenoteens